Arse Over Irish Teacup

JUDE MCLEAN

Also by Jude Mclean

Escape

Break Free

United

Anne Malloy

An O'Brian Bride For Christmas

Edited by Paula Demary

Published in the USA
ISBN: 9798883353870
Publisher: Jude McLean

www.judemclean.com

For Amanda with the adventurous soul.

CHAPTER

One

BETHANY SPINNER SIZED up the sassy and elegant red high heels perched on the floor by her bed. They were mocking her. Almost daring her to try, just try, slipping them on. With a determined nod she marched up to the strappy death-traps and grabbed one, wrestling open its tiny satin buckle. It was at that moment the little angel on her shoulder reminded her to sit down before going to battle with the red death-traps. But Bethany ignored that well-intentioned voice and declared that tonight would be the night she conquered the art of the one-legged shoe dance! She was an adult, for heaven's sake. And an accomplished nurse. Surely those qualifications would deem her more than equal to the task.

Now, for the hard part.

While standing up, she lifted her right foot and in her best Karate Kid pose, slipped on the shoe.

Ta-da! Bethany was still up! Take that!

She grabbed a hold of the second little devil and slowly raised her left foot—then swiped off the entire contents of her dresser top while toppling over. Her cherished vintage Strawberry Shortcake lamp stared at her with a dimpled smile as she somersaulted through the air and landed safely in Beth's outstretched hands.

"Bethany? Is everything all right in there?" Gram called out. She was the only one who used Beth's full first name.

"I'm fine, Gram. I'm just putting on my shoes," Beth called back. With a groan, she blew her hair away from her face, then got up from the floor and sat at the foot of her bed, catching her breath. Good thing she hadn't stumbled into that beast of a hope chest. How would that look on a first date? Good evening. Would you mind stopping at the emergency room before dinner?

Now if she could get those vexing straps out from between her toes.

After a few minutes of negotiations with her size eight demons, she was dressed and ready for her date.

Beth stood up, wobbled a little on the heels, smoothed her skirt, and pushed her hair out of her face. She would have pulled her hair back and up except she had learned long ago that bobby pins, hair sticks and anything else pointy near her face was a danger. Who would think you would actually need a bobby pin cut from your hair like a wad of bubble gum?

Beth touched the side of her hair, recalling how that had once been a bald spot. Bethany Spinner and Hubba Bubba didn't get along.

Beth leaned in to the full-length mirror and swiping her finger along her lower lip line, fixed her lipstick, then leaned back for one last check. Her loose, red curls were tamed as well as expected. No matter what she did, her hair was always a little frizzy, unless of course she plastered it with a hair product that could double as wallpaper paste. Ew. She turned left and right and looked at herself from head to foot. Her little black dress was a little snugger than it had been on her last date. No need to mention how long ago that was. But it still fit and still hugged all the right places. For a woman staring middle-age in the face, she looked pretty darn good, thank you very much.

Beth entered the family room where her ailing grandmother laid on the sofa under a blanket Beth herself had crocheted, looking at her husband's upside-down portrait on the wall. She looked tired. More tired than usual, but pointing that out wouldn't be at all helpful. Of course, Gram would look tired. That's what people who were dying looked like.

"What do you think, Gram?" Beth posed then wobbled on her high heels.

Gram examined Bethany from head to foot and softly smiled. Her granddaughter had been a beautiful baby, a beautiful teenager, and now she was a beautiful woman who was intelligent, perpetually optimistic, and kind, but God help her, she was the klutziest female ever to stumble across this earth. "You need something ..."

"Need what? More eyeshadow?"

"No, wait until you're my age and have a face like tree bark. Then you'll need more makeup. You look beautiful."

"Should I wear flat shoes instead? Do you think I'll trip?"

The odds of Beth tripping in those heels were most certainly high. But they looked great.

"Do you have to wear black?"

"Black goes everywhere, Gram. It's chic."

Chic, it may be, but her red-haired granddaughter looked best in green. "Bethany, you're a romantic to the core. That reminds me. I have something for you." Gram sat up on the couch and shooed Beth's hand away when she offered help. "It's in the top drawer of the hutch."

Beth smiled and opened the drawer to find a gift wrapped in silver paper with a green bow. By the feel, she knew it was a book, and she loved books. Excited to see what book it was, she tore it open, then gasped. A hardback edition of her favorite book!

"That paperback of yours has seen better days, so I thought you could use a backup copy." Gram had tried to contact the author to ask for a signed book but had never received a reply, but she wouldn't tell Bethany that.

"I love it, thank you!" Beth admired the cover, ran her fingers over the title, *Under the Irish Stars*. If she didn't put it down now, she would cancel her date and read it in one sitting. She placed the book down with loving care, and grabbed her purse from the hook on the wall.

"Why are you taking your large purse? Don't tell me—you have a book in there, don't you?"

Beth peeked in at her favorite paperback. The last date she'd had excused himself and never came back, and the one before that. Both before dinner had even been served. If this kept up, she was going to develop a complex! "If I get ditched again, I'm staying and finishing my dinner. I don't care if I'll be alone and reading while eating. That's preferable to spending an evening with a guy that doesn't like me. And since you won't let me cancel this date …"

"I'm going to die someday and when I do, I want to know you didn't miss a date for me." Gram pulled out the big guns to ensure she got her way. "It's my dying wish."

"You drive a hard bargain." She glanced at her wristwatch. "Lauren will be here any minute now."

"I don't know why you insist on her staying with me. I'll be fine for a couple of hours. You fuss over me too much."

"Because I won't be able to enjoy myself, knowing you're all alone. Lauren may not be a nurse but she won't let anything happen to you."

"What's going to happen to me? I can hardly put on my dancing shoes and sneak out like a thief into the night." Gram watched as Bethany walked across the room and wobbled again. Maybe those weren't such a grand idea after all. "Speaking of shoes. I'm not so sure you should wear those." Beth was going to sprain her ankle, she just knew it. "You have that lovely pair of flats with the rhinestone buckle."

"Not tonight, Gram. These go better with this dress."

"Hello?" Lauren called into the house from the front door, knocking as she opened it. She stepped inside and took off her sneakers as she called over her shoulder. "Gram, I hope you're ready for me. You and me are going to have a proper girl's night. I left the kids at home with Alan and I brought us *Pretty Woman* and *An Officer and a Gentlemen*, popcorn, and your favorite!"

She entered the family room holding up a bottle of Jameson 18 in one hand and the DVD's in the other.

"Lauren, she can't have whiskey!"

"Oh, come on Beth! What's it gonna hurt?"

"Yeah! I'm already dying. You think a little whiskey is going to do me in? Come here Lauren, honey." Gram held out her arms to bring the honorary family member in for a hug and kissed her cheek. "How are Alan and the boys?" One would never know Lauren was a lawyer right until her first baby was born. Then after becoming a mom, said she was fulfilled and wouldn't go back. She hadn't regretted it yet.

"All of them are good. The boys are all playing softball. So, Alan gets lots of father-son time in as their coach. He loves it."

Gram gave a thoughtful smile to Lauren. If anyone had told her that the unruly mouth named Lauren would grow up to be mother-of-the-year to three sons and wife to an adoring husband, all after becoming a lawyer, she would have never believed it.

"What will it be? Richard Gere with acrophobia or Richard Gere as an officer?"

"Officer. I never could say no to a man in uniform."

"You got it." She turned to Beth. "That dress looks amazing!" She lowered her gaze to Beth's shoes. "Those shoes look great too—but are you sure about wearing them?" Lauren had been a witness to several high-heeled hell incidents. That poor neighbor cat, it never walked right again.

"Good gracious! I think I can handle a pair of heels for one night. We're just going to dinner anyway, not for a hike."

Lauren shared a raised eyebrow look with Gram. Lauren would have an ice pack ready for when Beth returned. She took another look at the high heels and decided on two ice packs. Better to be safe than sorry.

"Who is this guy again?" Lauren asked.

"We met at the market. We both reached for the swiss chard at the same time and our heads bumped."

"Ew, he eats swiss chard? I don't like this guy," Lauren said.

"It's good for you."

"It's the most wretched, vile vegetable to exist. That and kale," Gram said. "Lauren, she tried to make me eat a smoothie with that garbage in it. That will kill me faster than a whiskey."

"Gram, I was only trying to—"

"I know what you were trying to do, and I love you for it. But Bethany, don't ever do it again. I'm old and dying and I'm not spending my last time here on earth drinking vile green juice."

Lauren reached into her bag and pulled out a square green Tupperware dish. That could only mean one thing.

"I smell chocolate chip cookies."

"I baked some fresh for you, Gram!" She opened the lid, releasing the aroma of baking.

Gram selected a cookie and smiled. "They're still warm. You're a good girl, Lauren. Thank you."

Lauren shared a smile with Beth. Gram could have anything she wanted so far as they were concerned. Beth may have expressed her concern over the whiskey, but that was only for show. It was more fun for Gram to have the things she shouldn't if she thought Beth didn't approve. But Beth would keep grasping any straw she could to buy her grandmother more time.

A car horn honked from the driveway. "What's that?" Gram asked. "Was there a car accident?"

Lauren went to the front window and looked out through the curtains. An obnoxious yellow sports car with a racing stripe down the middle blocked the driveway. Good grief. She would save the eye roll for after Beth left. "I think it's your date."

Beth joined her at the window and confirmed that it was him. "Wait until you meet him. He's got the most pretty blue eyes."

The two friends waited for the pretty blue eyes to emerge from the ugly yellow sports car. And waited. And waited.

"What sort of guy doesn't come to the door?" Lauren said. The jerk face could take his pretty blue eyes and shove it! Lauren didn't look convinced. Miffed, yes. But not convinced. Beth deserved a man that walked up to the damn door, rang the damn bell, and offered his damn arm to walk her to the damn car and then when they reached the damn car, open the damn door for her, dammit! Couldn't this guy see how special Beth was? Good luck finding a woman better than her because they aren't out there! You big fathead! *Breathe, Lauren.*

Beth got her purse and started for the door. "Maybe he's just nervous."

Lauren snatched a cookie and took a large bite. If she didn't, she was liable to storm outside and take a bite out of him. "Call if you need me to come get you. Where are you going anyway? And what's this guy's name?"

"Danny Scott. He's taking me to that new Italian restaurant on Third Street. Do you want to meet him? I can ask him to come inside."

Lauren and Gram looked at each other and in unison said, "No." He had no manners, an ugly car, and a first name for a last name. That was all they needed to know. At least they lived in a small town. This Danny wouldn't be able to pull anything without half the town knowing about it.

"Have a good time, and be careful in those shoes!" Lauren called to Beth as she walked out the door.

"I nearly forgot! I made a strawberry cake today." Beth called back over her shoulder.

Lauren followed her to the door to see her off. "With that fluffy, toasted coconut frosting I love so much?"

"Of course!"

"I love you! Have a good time! Just remember he won't buy the cow if you give the milk away for free, young lady!" Lauren teased in her mother-knows-best voice. She sighed and shook her head as Beth waved behind her while she walked, er, wobbled down the sidewalk.

"That's rich coming from you, Lauren. I caught you making out in my basement more times than I can count!" scolded Gram.

From the front door, Lauren watched her friend open her own car door and get into the ugly, striped lemon on wheels. Never mind that it was impractical for Minnesota, it was hideous! He hadn't even stepped out of the car to greet her outside. Nope. This guy wasn't the one for Bethany Spinner, but getting her out of the house for an evening was good. Maybe he would be a nice guy? If not, maybe Beth would meet someone better while out? The striped lemon peeled away with a squeal. Sigh … One could hope!

Lauren closed the door and returned to Gram. "Making out in the basement … those were good days. Remember Beth's first boyfriend?"

Who could forget poor Lars? He had a lazy eye, short mousy brown hair except for the tiny ponytail at the nape of his neck, and he could never be parted from that ridiculous cape. Gram nodded. "He was obsessed with that Dungeons and Dragons game. Remember the purple velvet cape he wore all the time?"

"And that rat's tail he sported? Lars still plays Dungeons and Dragons, works at Al's Pizza, and lives in his parent's base-ment." And right now he was preferable to Danny.

Lauren and Gram simultaneously rolled their eyes and laughed.

Lauren met Beth on the first day of kindergarten when, somehow, Beth got glue in her pigtails. Then the inevitable followed: glitter. Everywhere. Poor Beth looked like a disco ball with red curls springing out. Everyone, including the teacher, laughed at her, but not Lauren. Although it hadn't actually helped one iota, Lauren took Beth to the girls' room, soaped up her hair, and dunked her head under the running water in the sink. Unfortunately, it didn't work. Okay, so it made it worse, but that wasn't the point. The only solution was, of course, to cut Beth's left pigtail. And once the left pigtail was gone, Beth's hair looked stupid so naturally, the right had to follow. Lauren handled the hair removal personally. That was the day they learned that Bethany Spinner and glue were not compatible.

Incidentally, that was also the day they learned Lauren had no future in cosmetology.

They had been best friends ever since. And since that fateful day, Lauren had watched the revolving door of losers, all vying for Beth's heart. The trouble was they lived in a small town that didn't see many newcomers. Beth was running out of options.

The problem was that Beth was too nice. She saw the good in everyone—everyone. Even the guys that couldn't so much as get out of their damn ugly car and be a gentleman for three lousy seconds of their self-centered, pathetic lives. Buttheads! Breathe, Lauren.

"I'm going to get some cake. Would you like a slice?" Lauren asked.

"No, thanks, I had some earlier. I'll take another one of your cookies, though. I like chocolate with my whiskey."

"Want some tea with your whiskey?"

"No, straight up is good tonight."

Lauren went to the kitchen and returned with a pair of tulip glasses for the whiskey and a fat slice of pink cake with an equally fat scoop of vanilla ice cream. Tonight, she would eat through her rage aimed at the idiot man-child named Danny.

CHAPTER

Two

AFTER OPENING the restaurant door for herself, Danny had to answer a call on his phone. Beth sat down as the waiter pushed in her chair for her. At least someone around here had some manners, even if he was paid for them. The waiter paused a moment to look at Beth's soft face, and sweet expression, and wondered what sort of idiot would keep this angel waiting?

Right on cue, the idiot arrived, plopped down, and placed his cell phone on the table beside his napkin. Judging by the look of him, the waiter took the liberty of assessing that he was no doctor, fireman, or police and if he wasn't any of those and on call, then his juvenile yellow phone should be out of sight.

The waiter looked at Beth and said he would return with the wine list.

"Sorry. Work call."

That was a flimsy excuse to interrupt their date but Beth would forgive it. It was hard not to with the restaurant being so intimate with the candlelight, dark, rich colors, and romantic Italian dinner music. "That's okay. What is it you do?"

"I deal in fine antiques."

"That's interesting. How do you find the antiques?"

"I have a few contacts. Funeral homes and such. I also read the obituaries."

Beth's stomach rolled.

The waiter reappeared and presented Beth with the wine list, then practically tossed the list at Danny. Too bad he caught the menu.

Danny looked over the wine list. It couldn't be said that he read over the list because neanderthals rarely read, but without asking Beth what she might like, ordered a bottle of Chianti.

"So, who was that yelling at you when you were coming to the car?"

"Oh, that was my friend Lauren. She's watching Gram while I'm with you."

"Watching your grandmother?"

"Yeah, Gram has tuberculosis. It's a tricky disease, and she got it when she was a child, so it wasn't treated properly." Danny's eyes glazed over so she wrapped things up. "Anyway, I became a nurse so I could take care of her myself."

"Why? Couldn't you just put her in a home?"

Beth should have gotten angry, but she reminded herself that some people didn't understand. Gram had given up so much when she took Beth in after her parents died in that car accident. If there was anyone Beth would happily sacrifice herself for, it was Gram. But it wasn't a sacrifice at all.

"I don't agree. She took me in and raised me after my parents died. I haven't given up anything. I was and still am happy that I get to help her, be there with her. I'm not at all resentful." And she meant that with all her heart. Danny couldn't understand that. Beth enjoyed nursing. It meant she made a difference and helped people.

"So, how close is she to dying? Call me if you have anything you want to sell."

Beth blinked, unable to reply. It was moments like this when she wished she were more like Lauren. If she were, instead of sitting there mute, looking like a deer in headlights, she would have called him a meathead, thrown her water in his face and left. Thank the Lord for the waiter who appeared with the bottle of wine and poured Beth a glass first. She thanked him with a grateful smile, drank the entire glass then held it out for an immediate refill. This was going to be a long night.

————

"Okay, the game is Texas Hold Em. Deuces are wild," Gram said as she shuffled a deck of cards.

"I thought you wanted to watch a movie?"

"I'm old and entitled to change my mind."

Lauren, remembering another treat she had inside her purse sprang from her seat to retrieve the item. Gram smiled when Lauren returned with one of her favorite cigars.

A good cigar, a fine whiskey, and a game of poker. That's all Gram needed to be happy. She took the cigar from Laurens hand and ran it under her nose inhaling its fragrant aroma. Then placed it down on the table beside her glass. "I can't smoke this."

"Are you feeling okay?"

"I'm fine. Just a little more tired than usual is all. Nothing to worry about."

There were only two things Gram loved more than whiskey: Bethany and a good cigar. Lauren hid her concern like a pro. "That's okay, you can be like Elvis and just hold it between your teeth," Gram dealt the cards and Lauren sat examining her hand. "Funny the guy didn't come to the door to meet Beth."

"Yes, I don't like his name either. What grown man calls himself Danny? An arsehole if you ask me. But Bethany can take care of herself. If he's no good, she'll know and give him the heave ho."

"But that's only because that's all she dates. I'm afraid she won't know the real thing when it comes along! She shouldn't be left on the shelf!" Lauren whined.

"I know." Gram studied her cards for a moment then looked up. "Do you really think he eats swiss chard?"

"Nah. He was trying to get Beth's attention. Only puny yuppies would eat that rabbit food. And no puny yuppy would get the time of day from our girl."

"Thank the Lord for that."

"Lauren, my throat is as dry as a jockey's crotch."

In other words, Gram wanted a refill of whiskey. Lauren grinned and poured her another. Then nearly dropped the bottle when Gram made her play. "Pocket rockets, Gram? Seriously?" She slid Gram's glass across the table, then Lauren looked over her cards.

Gram took a sip of whiskey and another. "Are you going to play anytime soon? I am dying, you know."

"Keep your hair on, old woman."

"Don't lose hope. Bethany's life is about to change. I can feel it."

"It's not like you to be so mystical, Gram."

"I'm old and with age comes wisdom. I don't need your tarot cards to know that our Bethany will find love." Gram took another drink. "Now are you going to play or should I take a nap?"

CHAPTER
Three

BETH ARRIVED home to find Lauren watching the end of *An Officer and a Gentleman* by herself. Beth flopped beside her, swinging her feet over Lauren's lap.

Lauren unbuckled Beth's shoes and slipped them off her feet. "Do you need an ice pack?"

"No."

"You didn't trip? I'm impressed! My Beth is all grown up."

"Not quite. I did trip, but I fell into the waiter."

Familiar with what was coming next, Lauren cringed.

"I sort of made him drop his tray of clams." Beth sailed her hand through the air. "One landed in Danny's wine," Beth said with a laughing snort.

Just another night out with Beth. "So how was it?"

"I don't think he's going to call again which I won't mind. He was kind of a jerk. But something tells me you already knew that."

If Beth said he was "kind of a jerk" that meant he was a total schmuck. One of Beth's qualities, that was also her downfall, was that she believed the best in everyone. She wasn't naïve per se. She was trusting and focused on the good in people. It hadn't yet occurred to Beth that people were often jerks and didn't deserve her benefit of the doubt.

"I might have guessed but let's ask the cards."

Beth didn't believe in "asking the cards" but in the years of their friendship she had learned that when it came to Lauren's quirks it was better to just go with it.

Lauren returned with a new deck of tarot cards in her hand and sat down on the carpet on the opposite side of the coffee table. "I bought these in a moment of madness the other day."

Tarot cards with Disney characters on them. A moment of madness was right! Beth laughed as she shuffled and glanced at a few cards. Ursula, Captain Hook, Maleficent. Every villain Disney had all drawn in a dark, artistic fashion. Beth decided they were quite pretty, but she much preferred the look of Lauren's fairy-themed deck.

Lauren gave the cards a quick shuffle, then asked if Danny Scott was going to call again and flipped up a card. The Fool. Lauren knew he was definitely a fool. Most times the card would mean something like taking a leap of faith but she was going to take the card literally. No more cards needed to be flipped.

Beth chuckled. "Danny did all the talking. He's an estate ravager."

"A what?"

"He reads the obituaries and swoops in to buy up the estate of anything valuable."

"That would explain how he got the sports car. He probably snatched it from an old man living out his second childhood."

"Danny paid me a nice compliment just before insulting me.

He said I smelled sweet, and that I had the most beautiful face, but wondered if I had ever considered losing a few pounds."

"He what? That dickhead!"

"When our waiter came to take our order, he tried ordering for me: a tomato, mozzarella and basil salad. Not as an appetizer, but as my entrée. I told him I'm allergic to tomatoes, and that I was going to order the fettucine alfredo with grilled chicken. He said he's not jiggy with that. What does that even mean?"

"What is he, four? Beth, you have got to stop letting men treat you like this!" That irritated Lauren like nothing else.

"That's easy for you to say. You had the biggest attitude of anyone ever since we were kids! I remember the teacher taking roll call and when she asked your name you said, "none of your business!"

Lauren laughed. That was a good one. "How old were we?"

"That was the first day of kindergarten!"

"All I remember about that day is hair and glue." The two friends laughed at the memory.

"So, who won at Poker tonight? Did she smoke the cigar?"

"I won, and no," Lauren said slowly. Gram rarely lost a poker game. "She just held it between her teeth." Lauren sat beside Beth again on the couch and joined her arm with hers then laid her head on her shoulder. "It won't be long now, will it?"

"I don't think so." Beth put her arm around Lauren and stroked her brow for a minute. Although it was inevitable, neither wanted to think of a world without Gram in it. Enough of these thoughts! "I'm going to get out of this dress and have a slice of that cake. That restaurant served desserts the size of a scallop."

Beth peeked in on her grandmother as she passed her

bedroom. The room was dark, but with the light from the hallway flooding in, she could see the pink flowered wallpaper. Everything was quiet and Beth nearly turned away and closed the door, except it was almost too quiet.

"Lauren?" Beth called out as she approached Gram's bedside.

"Yeah?" When Beth didn't reply, Lauren got up from the sofa and came into the bedroom. "Something the matter?" Beth was taking Gram's pulse.

Beth turned to Lauren and slowly shook her head.

She placed Gram's hand at her side with loving care, kissed her forehead, then turned to Lauren, who was shaking her head as her tears fell. Lauren gathered Beth in her arms and held her tight as they shared their tears.

"Gram wouldn't want us crying like this, you know?"

Lauren nodded and wiped her teary eyes on her sleeve. There had to be tissues nearby. Lauren looked around the room and spotted a box on the dresser.

Beth nodded her head as she and Lauren slid to the floor beside the bed.

After a few minutes of hard bawling and nose blowing, the pair reminded themselves that this was not what Gram would have wanted.

"I'm going to miss my drinking buddy." Beth forced a chuckle through her tears.

That gave Lauren an idea. She blew her nose one more time before getting up and leaving the room, returning with the bottle of Jameson 18 and two fresh tulip glasses. Beth held onto the glasses while Lauren poured a drink in each, then they took a drink.

"Remember when she gave us our first drink?" Beth asked.

"New Year's Eve. We were thirteen, and she made us pink

squirrels. Then we both got sick, and she said to never forget that. We haven't."

"Yeah, pink squirrels are awful," Beth said. They clinked their glasses of whiskey. "Remember when she caught us making out with those two college guys?"

"I've never been so scared of another human being in my life."

"The guys were terrified!" They laughed some more. "Remember, they were falling over themselves trying to run away?"

"Yeah. Two brawny football players running scared!" Beth refilled her glass, then Lauren's, and took a long drink, which gave her a little too much time to think back. That football player may have been a sissy, but he'd been a great kisser.

Beth hadn't had a great kiss in a long time. Maybe it was her? Maybe she was the problem? She'd always believed Mr. Right was out there. She just hadn't met him yet. But what if he'd met her, witnessed a clumsy moment and split?

She stared blankly at the pink wall in front of her. "I've gained weight since taking care of Gram. I should lose a few pounds."

"Beth, you've always been happy no matter what size you were, so what's brought this nonsense around?"

"I have?" Beth considered it. "I have, haven't I!"

"You were born with an optimism gene. Sure, you have bad days like the rest of us, but they never get you down. Not really. This is your grief talking. Don't let this change you. You are curvy but you've got the nicest ass!"

"Lauren!"

"What? It's true. I couldn't get curves like yours no matter how hard I tried."

"You don't need curves, you're built like a supermodel."

"A supermodel who's given birth three times. Believe me, under this dress it's all sagging and scars and stretch marks."

"Now who sounds morose?"

"Don't you dare!" Lauren slapped Beth's shoulder. "It looks great on you. You've got the nicest ass now! Before you had a bony ass and a flat chest."

"I did? Why didn't you ever tell me?"

"Tell you what? 'Hey Beth, start eating more ding dongs so you pack on a few pounds?'"

Beth sighed. "And is it just my imagination or am I getting wings?" She held up her arm and shook it, and Lauren did the same.

"We both are. Age and gravity are catching up with us."

"Could it catch up a little slower, please? I still have unfulfilled dreams of a husband and family I want to come true."

"Don't worry about it. You look great. Nothing will change that. Not your weight, or wings. You're irresistible."

"Yeah, to all the wrong men."

"Your time is coming. I can feel it."

They fell silent for a minute. Forcing yourself to laugh through your tears is exhausting.

"Kind of like when you felt the shivers run up your spine when Jason Voorhees was in the window?"

"You were just as scared as I was! What child wouldn't be scared to hear scratching on their window only to turn around and see the face of pure, murderous evil itself!" Lauren threw back a drink. "How old were we?"

Beth swallowed another sip. "Nine."

"You know, come to think of it, Gram was a wicked cow."

Beth and Lauren both burst into laughter with Beth spewing whiskey all over the floor. Once she got control of herself, she raised her glass. "To Gram."

"She was a hell of a woman."

"She was the best."

Just then, Gram's hand slid off the side of the mattress, clunking Bethany on the head.

CHAPTER
Four

BETH WOKE up to the sound of cheerful chirping gold finches outside her window. She opened her eyes and blinked in the morning sun invading her room. Outside it was a beautiful Spring day. Normally the sound and sight would have made her smile but there wasn't much to make her smile this morning. All she wanted was for this day to be done and over with. She swung her legs out of bed and scratched her fingertips into her curls while she yawned fiercely. Tea, that's what she desperately needed. She stood up and put her arms through her yellow daisy-printed bathrobe and headed for the kitchen.

The house was too quiet.

Much too quiet.

Even the air was quiet.

She entered the kitchen and paused in the doorway. In her mind's eye she could see Gram standing at the stove, putting the kettle on and asking if Bethany wanted Irish Breakfast or blueberry tea that morning. Good gracious did she miss her.

She filled the kettle with water and placed it back on the

stove then selected a cup. From the assortment of flowers, and gag gift mugs she decided it was a "nope, not today" type of morning. She measured a spoonful of Blueberry tea into a bag, tied it up and dropped it into her cup, then opened the next cabinet and pulled down a plate. Eggs, toast, and tea was her usual breakfast and just because this was one of the worst days of her life didn't mean she couldn't at least enjoy her breakfast.

Beth dropped one egg. Of all the clumsy things she'd ever done, she had never, not once, dropped an egg. It was a sign. It must be.

Way to go, Beth. You ticked another one off from your 'never have I ever' list.

As the tea kettle whistled, she felt the icy hand of doom creep across her shoulders.

No, No, No! Not today! Bethany had never believed in giving in to despair and she would not start now. That wasn't what Gram wanted for her. She flipped her hair away from her face and poured the hot water into her cup, releasing the tea's fruity aroma. There, that was better.

After two cups of her favorite blueberry tea, two eggs, and two slices of toast with honey, she was fortified and ready to face the day.

But if those blessed goldfinches could knock it off for five flaming minutes?

––––––––

Beth stood in the living room staring outside the bay window. Across the street was an open field whose tall green grass was dabbled with wild flowers, bordered by a forest. Outside it was still a bright Spring day. And still too bright. Couldn't nature see she was in mourning? Couldn't it for just one day be dreary?

One day? Is that really too much to ask for? She turned away, letting the curtains fall closed behind her.

She looked at her wrist to check her watch and realized she hadn't put it on. There was no need to know the time consistently now that Gram was gone. The grandfather clock struck eleven, shattering the silence. Its gong was so loud she swore it reverberated inside her rib cage. She looked over at the clock as it continued to strike. Surely it must have gonged one hundred times by now.

Between the blazing sunshine, the chorus of birdsong, and the gong of the clock, her head was ringing. She rubbed her temples and behind her ears and breathed long and steady. Okay. Ready.

The ladies from Gram's church group would arrive to coordinate the wake and Lauren would arrive any minute now to pick her up. Right on time as usual, the doorbell rang.

Beth opened the door. "Since when do you ring the doorb—" she stopped short, holding the doorknob. The door only half open.

"Sorry, should I have knocked instead?" asked Danny.

Why, no! We don't expect common courtesy around here!

He was the last person she'd expected to see on her doorstep. It's not like their date was a raving success. But here he was. "Hi, no, sorry. I thought you were someone else." She opened the door wide and stepped aside, allowing him to pass. "You must have seen the obituary."

"No, well, I might have, but you never told me your grandmother's name. Why, has she died?"

"Today is her funeral."

"I had no idea her funeral was today. I swear." Even he didn't buy his story. He waited for her to forgive him because Beth was like that. When she said nothing, he waited for another awkward moment then continued. "I'm sorry for your loss." He patted her shoulder in an atta girl sort of way. "Also, I found this in my car." He held up her book. "It must have fallen out of your purse …" Or he might have taken it from her purse to use as an excuse to see her again after the old woman died. "Do you always go on a date with a book in your bag?"

"Yes, but it's nothing personal." So, he hadn't known today was Gram's funeral? Yeah right. He'd had an entire week to return her book.

"This book has seen better days. Why don't you toss it?"

"Because it's my favorite!" She snatched it from his hand and clutched to her chest. This day was bad enough, must she lose her book too? "Thank you for bringing it to me."

"I read the back cover. Why do you read that garbage?"

She blinked twice. First in disbelief then because she couldn't stop the tears rushing in. She looked at the floor and closed her eyes. Everything was quiet, except for her racing heart and the goldfinches who were still going strong, until Lauren's voice rang from outside.

"Beth? Somebody's ugly BMW is blocking your driveway. I left them a note telling them to move it or it will be towed. Some people are so inconsiderate. God, my pantyhose are so twisted, I'm walking like John Wayne," Lauren called out as she wobbled through the corridor. She walked through the house and into the living room, where she found her best friend staring at the floor, clutching a book like a life preserver. Lauren laid a hand on Beth's arm. "Beth? What's going on?"

"It's my fault. I teased her about her book," explained Danny.

Lauren's concerned eyes snapped away from Beth to the source. Let's see, ugly car and pretty blue eyes. It could only be Danny Scott. She tested what he was really made of. He was already at the bottom of her list. Nobody teased her best friend and got away with it. "And just who the hell are you?"

"I'm Danny with the ugly BMW."

The arrogant jerk hadn't even flinched. And exactly how many ugly cars did one person need? She propped her fists on her hips. "Danny, move your car."

"It's okay, Lauren. I'm fine," said Beth. She wiped her eyes and put on her best brave face.

"Fine? None of us are fine." Lauren elbowed past Danny. Not because she needed to but for the sheer pleasure of it. "We aren't supposed to be fine. Not today. You sit down for a couple minutes while I get the portrait. Everything else is all set. Do you need help with anything or are you ready to go?"

Beth nodded her head as she emptied her lungs. "I'm ready as I'll ever be."

"Do you want a cup of tea before we leave? We have time."

"No, I'm all right. Let's just get the picture and get going."

Lauren shoved a chair in front of the fireplace then climbed on, trying to get portrait down from the wall but it was stuck. Danny stood there looking the other way with his hands in his pockets probably eyeing the silver. What a gentleman. "Hey, Danny with the ugly BMW, stop standing there looking like you're waiting for a message from God and lend me a hand with this."

He looked to the fireplace and scrunched his brow. Hanging above it was a portrait of a man that hung upside down. He was about to ask about why it hung that way but worried what the answer would be. What sort of kooky family was this anyway? He got the picture down then asked where she wanted it.

"In the back seat of my car that's parked behind yours—if it's not too much trouble." Lauren suspected that most things would be too much trouble for Danny boy.

"No problem." He lifted the portrait and carried it outside, placing it on the back seat.

Lauren and Beth came through and Beth locked the door behind her.

"Do you want to ride over with Danny?" Lauren asked.

"Ride? Where?" Danny asked.

"To the church." Lauren answered then turned her attention back to Beth. "Why don't we have Danny follow us? Drew has the kids in the other car so it will be just us."

Beth nodded.

"The funeral is at Saint Mary's on Pringle Street. Do you know it?" Lauren asked Danny.

"Yeah, I know it."

"Okay, we'll see you there."

Danny didn't dare to argue. If he wasn't mistaken, there was an authentic Fabergé egg inside the china cabinet. So if attending the old broad's funeral was the price for that egg, so be it. He hustled to get his BMW out of the way before Lauren-the-ball-buster rammed it.

Lauren opened the car door for Beth and held it as she got in. "I don't know about this one, Beth. He has that sideways mouth talking thing and has a cocky smirk." Bethany got in and chuckled for a brief second. "Then again, he showed up today. I have to hand it to him."

Beth didn't mention the pretense he'd used. After all, maybe he felt he'd need a good excuse to offer his sympathies. Not all men were comfortable with situations like this.

CHAPTER
Five

"BETH?" Lauren cried. "My God! Are you okay?" Somehow Beth had ended up at the bottom of an open grave. Lauren wanted answers, but first she needed to get her out of there. "Are you hurt?"

"No, I'm okay. Just shaken up."

Lauren sat on the edge of the gaping six-foot hole and reached for Beth's hands. The two friends clasped hands and Lauren pulled. "What happened?"

"He just dumped me!" Beth started climbing the dirt wall of the grave. "He only showed up today so he could case Gram's house!"

"What?" Lauren roared.

Poor Bethany, who was halfway out of the hole, was dropped. But with her fists balled and snarling with the strength of her rage, Lauren plucked Beth out as if she were a feather. Then whirled around to Danny.

He'd managed a little preliminary research on the possible Fabergé egg only to turn up disappointing results. As for what else he saw, sure there were a few pieces of silver but nothing in the house was worth the hassle. Now, he had a raging lunatic in his face. "I—I—"

"You're pathetic!" Lauren lunged, warning him. "You and your stupid, ugly sports cars! This is Minnesota, land of snow, ice and salt! How long can you drive them? A month? I've got news for you shithead, Beth wouldn't sell so much as a single spoon to you! Now, you've got two choices. You can walk away or you can limp away! I'll count to three!"

He jumped back, shielding himself with his hands. "Okay, okay, easy! I didn't want to upset her! I thought I'd be able to slip away and she wouldn't ever see me again!"

Lauren had heard enough. Never taking her eyes off Danny lest he try to escape, she replied. "Did you hear that, Beth? He was just going to slip away! Really, that was so thoughtful. You'll have to excuse my friend Beth here. She's grieving her dead grandmother, so, please, allow me to reciprocate your consideration on her behalf." Before Danny knew what hit him, Lauren shoved him into the grave and grinned when he hit the ground with a thud. Lauren stood, bent over, pointing her finger at Danny cowering in the corner. "You shithead! You're as manly as tits on a bull! I'd like to feed your family jewels to the squirrels! How dare you!" Lauren turned to leave, then turned back. "I hope rats slowly gnaw away that stupid sideways mouth of yours! And the crows peck out your eyes! And snakes slither into every orifice as you rot in that grave!" She turned away again, took two steps, then turned back. "And it's your loss, buddy! Not only is Beth the best woman on earth but she can suck the nails out of a board!"

Danny, with the pretty blue eyes and ugly car, had had a plan. A good one. No, a brilliant one. Wait until the funeral service was underway, then quietly excuse himself, sneak out the back, and make a break for it.

The plan was flawless.

It should have worked.

Well, if his plan had been so brilliant and so flawless, then how did he end up here—crying like a baby from the bottom of an open grave?

I'll tell you how. He ignored the klutzy woman and underestimated the gutsy one!

As he stared up at the blue sky from the bottom of the six-foot worm-infested hole, he replayed the event in his head and decided the moment that everything really, ahem, went south, was when he'd chosen to be a nice person. That never paid off.

All the proceedings were over and he had been about to make a break for it when Beth wandered off alone into the cemetery. Some old bitty asked him to go after her. What had he done? Not what he'd wanted to do! He'd wanted to get into his BMW and blow that popsicle stand but he went after Beth.

Beth placed her arm around Lauren's shoulders, easing her away from the edge of the gaping hole before she could leap in like a rabid dog. "Okay, Big Hoss. Settle down."

"Settle down? Beth, that asshole was casing your house! And he just dumped you! At Gram's funeral! Then he left you! At. The. Bottom. Of. A. Grave! I believe I'm entitled to be a little upset!"

Beth eyes widened. There in the center of her iris, a flicker. "You're right." She thought for another moment, staring at nothing. Then her eyes snapped into focus. "You're right! I am entitled to be upset!" her words grew louder and louder. "I'm upset that Gram died! I'm upset that I have to go through this alone! I'm upset that these stupid birds won't give it a rest! And I'm upset that I didn't shove that, that—" Beth needed a little help with this rave.

"Dickhead."

"That DICKHEAD into that grave myself!"

It should be pointed out that Bethany Spinner seldom used vulgar language, but today, in the middle of the cemetery surrounded by stone edifices and memorials, she swore so loud that Lauren was pushed backward by the gust. Beth hadn't ever yelled that loud before. In. Her. Life.

Lauren waited for the echoing to stop. "How did that feel?"

Bethany smiled as she huffed and puffed. "Great!"

Lauren took a very deep breath and hugged her friend into her side as they walked toward the car and undoubtably the crowd of people waiting to give Beth an applause for as they say, finally letting it all "hang out."

The friends strolled arm in arm while somewhere in the not-so-distant distance, screeches sounding like a little girl wailing drifted on the breeze. What a pleasing sound.

"I love bird song, don't you? It's so soothing and pleasing to the ear," Beth said as she hugged Lauren's arm tighter. "That was an impressive speech you gave. Where on earth did that sucking nails from a board bit come from?

I don't know. Maybe I read it in a book or something." Lauren gave Beth a sideways look, and the pair burst into giggles. "Now, are you ready for the wake, or would you like to get drunk first?"

"No, I think I'm ready. Gutsy, where would I be without you?"

"You would still be in that grave for starters."

CHAPTER
Six

LAUREN HAD HEARD ENOUGH of the mid-west goodbyes. "No, I insist ... That's all right, it's unnecessary ... I won't hear of it ..." and the backhanded insults. It was time for everyone to go home. Besides, all the "sorry for your loss" wishes were followed with "now you can find a husband. You still have time ..." That was it! Lauren had heard enough. Beth had time! She deserved happiness! She'd earned it! All these "well-wishers" had earned was a slap in the face and a kick in the backside for being so rude.

Somewhere there was a kind man waiting for Beth to trip into his arms. She just hadn't tripped into them yet. Lauren was reminded of the time Beth fell off a ladder right into the waiting arms of Jacob Olson. He was tall, dark, handsome, and the top of their class. He was also the most boring bore of all the bores in all of Minnesota.

Thank you for coming. Yes, we all miss Gram. Bub-bye now. Don't let the door hit you on the way out.

Having herded everyone outside, Lauren closed the door and turned the lock.

Beth thanked Lauren for coming to her rescue, then turned toward the living room. The soft sofa was calling her name.

"Thank God that's all over. The ladies from church are nice and all, but they're tyrants!" Lauren looked around. Tyrants they may be but at least they had gone through the house like a white tornado, leaving no trace of their presence except a refrigerator stuffed with food, bouquets of flowers and a basket of sympathy cards. "You know what you need? A long, hot shower. Then get into your pajamas."

"You must be tired, too. Why don't you go home to Alan and the boys? I'll be fine tonight."

"Are you kidding? Pass up the chance to have an entire bed all to myself? No way. Besides, Alan wants me to stay and get you drunk."

Alan was probably the nicest guy in the world, not to mention the world's best husband. Lauren had offered to stay with Beth every night since Gram passed away but Beth wouldn't let her. But tonight, after the hardest day of her adult life, she was grateful for the company.

Beth got up from the sofa and stretched her neck from left to right. A long, hot shower did sound ever so good and a hot whiskey sounded even better. With no more fuss, she made her way to the bathroom, then paused when she saw her favorite paperback resting on the side table. She touched her fingertips to its tattered cover, then continued on her way.

"Now, get in that shower. I don't want to see you for at least twenty minutes."

"What am I supposed to do for twenty minutes in the shower?"

"Wash that hellcat hair of yours three times to get that grave dirt out, for starters. When you come out, I'll have hot whiskeys for both of us."

While Beth showered, Lauren put the kettle on and sliced a lemon. The bright scent of the freshly cut lemon felt wrong on a day like today, but right somehow. She poked whole cloves into the extra thick lemon slices. That was the secret to a good hot whiskey. They had never heard of hot whiskeys until Beth had read that book, *Under the Irish Stars*.

That got Lauren thinking. Which got her thinking about Beth's love life, or the lack thereof. Which got her thinking about Danny. Which then made her mad and want to spit. Beth is too nice! She always has been! But do people appreciate that about her? Of course not! Suddenly Lauren's feelings came flying out of her mouth and right out loud she hollered, "Men walk all over her and she's so damn trusting!"

"What?" Beth called out from inside the shower.

"Nothing! I just turned on the TV!" Lauren quickly found the remote and turned on the television. It didn't matter what program played so long as it was on. She hated lying to Beth. Even a little white lie felt like a betrayal.

Shaking her head, Lauren placed the remote down beside Beth's book. Ever since Beth read it, she always had a copy with her. For some, it was an American Express card they never left home without, for Beth, it was this Irish romance novel.

That was six years ago.

Lauren picked up the book and flipped through its worn pages. Six years of Beth being in love with a story but never being in love. Enough was enough.

If Lauren had anything to say about it, Beth was going to find herself an Irishman who adored her, and they were going to live happily ever after and that was all there was to it! But getting Beth to go would take a little finesse. Finesse wasn't exactly Lauren's specialty. This was going to require some thought.

The teapot whistled, summoning Lauren to the kitchen to finish making the drinks. She placed the lemon slices into the cups, then fetched the bottle of Jameson and as she poured the golden whiskey, was reminded of the important papers inside her purse.

Lauren finished preparing the drinks, set the bottle aside, and fetched her purse just as Beth appeared in the kitchen freshly showered, and looking cute in her flannel Garfield pajamas.

"Do you feel a little better?" Lauren asked as she handed Beth her drink.

Beth took a sip of the warm whiskey and let it slide down her throat, nodding her head. "You made this perfect, thank you."

With the papers in hand Lauren suggested they take their drinks and relax in the living room.

Lauren sat at one end of the sofa and patted her lap instructing Beth to lay down and place her feet there.

Once Beth was comfortable and had finished half of her drink Lauren handed over the two envelopes. "Gram gave these to me a few months ago and asked me to save them for after she was gone. It's her will and a letter. She left everything to you."

Beth unfolded the will and tried to read it but the legal jargon was too much for her frayed wits, so she folded it back up and placed the will back inside its envelope. She was much more interested in the letter anyway but when it came down to it, she didn't have it in her to read that either. "I always thought she would leave most of it to the church."

"That's what this will says. It's not enough to let you sit on your ass the rest of your life, but it will keep you comfortable."

"Have you read the letter?"

"No, I haven't. Do you want me to read it to you?"

"No, not tonight. I've cried enough tears today. Is that okay?"

"Of course it is." Lauren rubbed Beth's foot with her free hand. It had been a long, long day. Whatever Gram's last words to Bethany were, they could wait.

The two friends stared blankly at the television where a rerun of Buffy the Vampire Slayer played. This was not ideal. Lauren took the remote and cruised through the channels, stopping on a travel show where a couple was strolling down a white sandy beach.

"That beach looks wonderful," said Beth.

"You know, Gram left you enough that you could take a long break. Do something for yourself. And only for yourself."

"But there's nothing I want to do."

"What about going to Ireland? You've always wanted to do that and remember Gram left it all to you. You could stay as long as two or even three months."

"But, you're suggesting I practically move there."

"No, I'm not. Just an extended vacation. You could drive around, stay wherever you want for as long as you like. Think of the freedom you would have. We can make it open-ended so that you can come home whenever you're ready." Lauren saw a spark in Beth's eyes so she continued. "Come on. Maybe you will find a hot Irishman with sparkling blue eyes? And you could find the places from your book. How romantic would that be if you met someone and went to see one of those places?"

Sold! One ticket to Ireland, please. No return date.

"What am I going to do without you in Ireland?"

"You'll be just fine. And you never know, I might visit."

"Do you ever think I'll find what you and Alan have?"

Lauren and Alan were the happiest couple Beth had known. Sure, they fought, but they fought and made up as a team. Alan adored her and his children.

"Let's ask the cards!" Perfect. This couldn't have worked out better!

Lauren skipped away to fetch her trusty tarot cards. She sat on the floor on the opposite side from Beth and handed them over for Beth to shuffle.

"I want to know if that low-life cockhead is still whining from the bottom of that grave! If there were any justice in this world, zombies would be real and Danny would be their dinner right now."

Lauren began the reading making up meanings to the cards, saying Beth needs a change. "And lookee there, Captain Hook and Smee agree!" Lauren flipped up another card, didn't care for it so pulled another. "I still cannot believe you fell into a grave."

"I know."

"I mean, a grave. Beth, that's got to be the worst ever."

"Is this supposed to make me feel better?"

"Sorry. You know, I think he actually peed his pants."

"No way!"

"I swear I saw a wet spot on his pants just before you pulled me away."

"How many boys does this make that you've made cry?"

"Eight?"

"No, eight was the bag boy last Thanksgiving," Beth said as she popped a chocolate in her mouth. "Remember? You nearly threw a whole turkey at him."

"Don't look at me like that. He put the turkey on top of the bread. What sort of idiot does that? I did that potato-head a favor, yelling at him. How else was he going to snap out of it?"

Beth stared at the white sandy beach pictured on the television. It did look inviting. "But I can't just up and go to Ireland."

"Why not? Who's stopping you?"

"Nobody."

"That's right, so quit yakking and start packing."

CHAPTER
Seven

"CRIPES, BETH!" Lauren strained to catch a breath after heaving the red suitcase down the sidewalk to the car. "Why didn't we think to go shopping for luggage?" she bent over resting her hands on her knees.

"Do they still have helpers at the airport?"

"Helpers? Are you kidding me? I forget sometimes how long it's been since you've really been anywhere."

"What are you talking about? We go on a girl's trip twice a year."

"Yeah, but we haven't flown anywhere in ages. And you've never brought along this beast. I would have remembered that."

"It was Gram's. I couldn't find my luggage."

"I figured." Lauren groaned. "Well," One last shove and it would be in the trunk. "This way Gram gets to go with you." Thud. Lauren stood up and, with a smile, wiped her brow with the back of her hand. "She'd like that!"

"I thought of that too." Beth wiped a tear from the corner of her eye. "Gram would have loved this."

Beth stepped outside onto the landing and closed the door behind her then locked it and turned for the car where Lauren was leaning against the car guzzling a bottle of Coke. She chugged the whole thing then dropped the bottle from her lips and belched.

Beth shook her head. "You are nothing but a picture of gentle feminity."

Lauren belched again, only smaller this time. "What?"

It wouldn't take a genius to figure out that Lauren lived in a household of all boys and had her entire life. Beth smiled and said, "I won't be here to give you your daily dose of estrogen. By the time I get back you'll probably be wearing a hockey jersey everywhere you go, and wipe the beer from your mouth with your sleeve while stuffing pretzels in it at the same time."

"Are you calling me a neanderthal?"

"Sort of. I'll know you're beyond hope if you stop wearing all your necklaces." Lauren loved her silver necklaces.

Lauren struggled not to cry as she laughed. Beth needed to go, deserved to go. Lauren knew that. But damn if she wasn't going to miss her. She gathered Beth in to her arms and rocked her hard in a hug. "All set to go?"

"Ready as I'll ever be."

"Don't look so scared. It's all going to be great!"

Famous last words.

———

Beth dropped her bank vault, er ahem, suitcase, onto her foot. She really should have bought new luggage. She could have just brought along Gram's picture and that wouldn't have crushed her foot!

Once she'd hugged Lauren once more and wiped a few tears,

she waved to the car pulling away then turned, heaved up her suitcase with both hands and walked through the airport sliding doors.

And tripped.

Into a man.

"Ope! I'm so sorry!" she cried as she balanced herself on a pair of powerful arms and stood up.

"Watch where you're going!"

He had yet to stand so she couldn't see the man's face yet but what little she saw was turning red. When he straightened and looked at her, she froze. Her eyes locked with eyes of the deepest pool blue staring at her with boiling irritation.

"Would you mind removing your case from my foot?" he growled.

She snapped out of it. "Oh, no! I'm sorry! So sorry! Oh, good gracious!" She was so flustered she didn't know what to do first.

"You know, they make barges to carry this size suitcase! If you can't handle it on your own, then you shouldn't have brought it!"

She gripped hold of her suitcase with both hands and lifted it from his foot, then dropped it beside her. Thud. "Listen, I'm sorry that I ran into you, but I didn't do it on purpose and you're fine!" she spat. Where had that come from? Did she just say that? Not believing that was her raised voice, Beth shrunk. "You are fine, aren't you?"

He circled his foot. "Yes." He almost sounded disappointed. "What's your point?"

Her point? Um, what was her point? She had lost her concentration looking at him. Good gracious, one would think she'd never seen a handsome face before. Danny had been handsome and look where that had gotten her. Enough of this. Earth to Bethany! "The point is I've apologized—genuinely. Profusely! I really am very sorry for running into you and dropping my suit-case on your foot. It hurts, I know, I dropped it on myself a few minutes ago and I'm really sorry, but you don't have to be so ..." So handsome. "So mean about it!"

"Ouch," he said in a dry voice. "Do you want the knife back or should I leave it in my heart?"

The clumsy woman with the big brown eyes looked as if she might burst into tears. His cynical side had come out in full force. Way to go, jerk wad. She didn't deserve that.

Before Beth saw his expression soften, she grabbed hold of the suitcase handle once again and marched away practically dragging the case behind her.

He struggled with whether or not to help her.

His foot throbbed.

He should help her.

Of course, he should. Come on, he wasn't raised in a barn!

He dithered too long. The clumsy woman was placing the red beast onto the scale at the check-in counter with the help of an older male attendant who was clearly besotted with her.

He watched the exchange as other passengers were inconve-nienced, forced to walk around him standing in the middle of the terminal like a pillar of salt. He caught himself smiling as he observed her rummaging through her purse. The attendant was smiling too—especially wide as she bent over to chase after a small bottle rolling across the floor. When she triumphantly caught the bottle, he shook his head with a grin and walked away.

"Good thing I caught up with these! I can't fly without them." She opened her palm to produce the small bottle of medication.

"Now, you're all set Miss Spinner. This is your boarding pass. Keep this and your passport handy because you're going to need it at security." The attendant pointed to his left to the security line. "So, your first trip to Ireland. That's exciting."

"Is it exciting? I know it should be. I'm waiting to be excited. Right now, I'm really nervous."

"Don't you worry. A pretty little thing like you, if you need help all you will have to do is flutter those eyelashes of yours and flash that smile. Now, don't forget, after you get through security there is a first-class lounge. Just follow the orange signs that will be to your right."

"That lounge sounds nice. I've never flown first-class before."

"What better time to splurge than on a twelve-hour flight, too. You won't be sorry. In the lounge there's a free bar and buffet, private washrooms, recliners, and it's always quiet." Since he was at least twenty years older than Beth, he knew this exchange needed to wrap up. Although he would have happily detained this charming woman for as long as possible. "So, is there anything else I can do for you?"

"I guess not. Thank you," Beth said, in an unsure but determined voice.

By the time she spotted the entrance to the lounge she assumed she had just trekked through half of the airport. Scads of people were walking in every direction, some fast some painfully slow and some even stood in place causing a stop in the foot traffic. Everyone was staring at their phone screen instead of where they were walking. She was nearly trampled twice, by no fault of her own, which threw her into a rack of Minnesota Wild sweatshirts. Both she and the rack stumbled to the floor but did anyone offer help? No.

Oh well, they all had flights to catch too. She dusted herself off and sprung up. When she swept the hair back, she couldn't have been more pleased to see the door to the lounge staring her in the face.

Thank goodness.

The door opened, she stepped inside, and like magic, all the noise and hustle and bustle stopped. Inside, the lounge was quiet and the people in it were in no hurry to get anywhere, except maybe the bar.

Beth approached the small bar where a bartender who looked barely old enough to be drinking himself was pouring drinks for a couple. While waiting, she looked around and spied a quiet corner near the window. That's where she would take her drink.

"What can I get for you miss?"

"Could I have a whiskey sour, made with Jameson if you have it, please? And a little on the sweet side?"

"Coming right up." The boy smiled and went to work.

It surprised her when instead of pouring simple whiskey sour mix, he poured egg whites into a shaker, followed with lemon juice, bitters, syrup and ice. He shook up the ingredients then with a flourish, poured the mixture into a glass and topped it with a perfect spiral of lemon.

Beth took a sip and exhaled with a smile on her lips. It was perfect. A girl could get used to this first-class thing. She thanked him, left a generous tip, then turned for that cozy corner by the window.

Then again, she should eat a little something with her drink. She didn't need to be plastered.

Beth turned back towards the buffet. And crashed into a body.

"Oh, good gracious! I'm sorry!" she cried as her perfect whiskey sour was relocated onto someone's shirt. She looked up and gasped. "You!"

"You."

Beth tore her eyes away from the familiar, gorgeous but blazing mad blue ones of the man whose foot she had crushed. Gulp.

"This seems to be a habit of yours." For so many reasons, he was so not amused. Her perfect lemon twist fell from his chest to the floor.

"I'll find napkins and—" Oh dear. His shirt was soaked, her airy foam scattered everywhere. This would require a lot of napkins. She hurried to the bar and the bartender, having witnessed the catastrophe, already had a towel ready. But when she turned back the man and her drink were storming away for the men's room.

Looking like she had just run over a puppy, she returned the bartender his towel.

"Can I make you a fresh whiskey sour? I'll make it a double, and on the sweet side. Maybe extra foam?" She hadn't answered before he was pouring egg whites again.

Dressed in a clean, dry shirt, the angry man stepped out from the men's room and scanned the lounge. No sight of the walking disaster. Seeing as the coast was clear he made his way to his usual corner seat. Nobody ever bothered him there.

Except *her*.

There she was, the pretty klutz, sitting in his chair, in his corner, beside his window. Did she not see the sign, "No girls allowed?"

Okay, so there was no such sign. So what? She was still in his seat.

Was there any place he could go to get away from her? Irritated, he turned around to find another seat as far away from her as possible!

"Oh! I was hoping I would run into you again." Poor choice

of words. "Wait, please?" She stood up with her arm outstretched.

She'd spotted him. Dammit. "Would you like to spill something on my pants? Run over my dog? Break my nose?" That was harsh and he knew it. And the minute he had spoken those words he felt sorry for it.

"Good gracious no, I only wanted to apologize—"

"Again."

Jeez Louise he would not make this easy. "Yes, again. I'm sorry." She waited a beat for him to say something but he didn't. Okay, she could make her own gesture of goodwill. "Can I at least buy you an I'm-sorry-for-spilling-my-drink all-over-you drink?"

"And for dropping your suitcase on my foot?"

"And for dropping my suitcase on your foot," she said in a dry voice. Her own throbbing foot reminded her that she had dropped a very heavy case on him. "Your foot's still okay?"

Seeing that her concern was genuine, he eased up. "It doesn't need to be amputated. You might have ruined my dreams of ever becoming a ballerina though."

Bethany grinned at the sarcasm. It was just the sort of remark her grandmother would have made. The thought made her heart ache and eyes burn with tears wanting to fall.

"It's a free bar."

"That's right. I forgot." Beth looked away and sniffled. She would not cry! This was not the way she imagined her vacation of a lifetime would begin.

His tone softened at the sound of her sniffles. "Listen, it's fine. See? Look." He stood on one foot shaking the other. She looked up at him with tears threatening to fall at any moment.

He ran his hand through his hair. He needed to make peace with her. "You already have a drink. How about I get my own and join you?" There. A quick drink to smooth things over. Then he wouldn't ever have to see her again.

Beth figured that meant he was going to walk away and not come back and who would blame him? She nodded her head with a weak smile.

And was utterly shocked when two minutes later he returned with a bloody Mary in his hand.

He sat beside her in a seat that was more like an armchair than a typical hard, airport seat. Between them was a small round table where he would not place his drink because the purpose of this conversation was to make sure he hadn't crushed this woman's spirit with his cruelty.

He stirred his Bloody Mary with the celery stick and took a long, refreshing drink. There. That was better. He looked at the whiskey sour in her hand. "The bartender used too many egg whites in your drink." Typical young bartenders. It didn't matter where the bar was, they were all the same: Put a pretty face in front of them and they all go stupid.

"He did that special for me. The foam is my favorite part and after he saw what I did to you, thought I could use a little extra foam. Nice guy."

"I told him my favorite part is the vodka but he didn't add extra."

She grinned. "I guess this just isn't your day."

He allowed a small outburst of laughter. "You could say that. So, what's your name?"

"Bethany Spinner. Most people call me Beth."

"I'm Aidan Turner. Nice to meet you, Beth." Part of him wanted to offer his hand in greeting but he ignored the urge.

As soon as he relaxed, she did too and they fell into simple conversation. "Did that hurt just now? Saying it was nice to meet me?"

He shook his head with a smirk and took a sip of his drink. "Are you traveling for business or pleasure?"

"Pleasure. You?"

"It's more like a family obligation and I'll use my work as an excuse to avoid as much contact with the family as possible."

"Really? I can't imagine wanting to hide from my family. Although, I don't have much family so I guess I'm not the best reference. What's the obligation?"

"My sister is getting married," he took another deep sip of his drink, "again."

"How many times has she been married?"

"This will be husband number four. I believe his name is Jimmy. There was Bono, and her first was Skip." He thought for a minute. "I can't remember the other one's name. It didn't last long enough to remember. I think she just trolls around for men with the dumbest names on earth. What sort of grown man calls himself Jimmy?"

Beth knew what sort but why mention that now?

"So, where are you flying to?" Aidan asked.

"Ireland."

He spit a little then wiped the burning tomato juice from his eye. "Flying into Dublin or Shannon?" He hoped the horror creeping up his spine hadn't reached his face. Surely, she would fly to Dublin. People loved Dublin. They didn't know there was anywhere in Ireland but Dublin.

"Shannon. Where are you going?"

"Shannon." Oh, dear God. Had anyone else heard that? That unmistakable sound of the earth cracking wide open, and laughing?

He certainly wasn't 2.3 seconds away from a panic attack.

He was fine.

She was fine.

Everything was going to be fine.

No worries!

Even if she was seated beside him, surely, he could change seats. He'd made this trip dozens of times. These flights were never full.

CHAPTER
Eight

"I'M SORRY, sir. That flight is full."

Sorry? She was sorry? Did the dingbat even know what she had just said?

He was fine.

He certainly wasn't having a heart attack or a stroke—no matter how much it felt like he was. Aidan leaned forward with both hands gripping the counter, pleading his case to the young bimbo poorly disguised as an air-headed agent. The next thing he knew the room was spinning.

He closed his eyes and shook his head, then slumped away back to his corner. But it wasn't his corner. Not anymore. It was Beth's corner. Sure, she was sharing with him but she was there. In his space. Spilling, crying, and dropping things. Sure, she was sweet, not to mention beautiful, but for God's sake could she go ten blazing minutes without maiming him or herself?

He rounded the corner and stopped. There she was. Bethany, who most people called Beth, with her peaches-and-cream skin, rosy, heart-shaped lips, bright smile, wide, honey-brown eyes, and hellcat hair that seemed incongruent with her innocent nature. She was staring out the window, clutching her drink. Her pretty face was scared but determined. He turned back for the bar, downed a shot of whiskey, ordered another and downed that too, then headed back to Beth.

So what if he was stuck with her for the twelve hour flight to Ireland? Big deal? How bad it could possibly be? I mean what damage could she do, really, when confined to a seat? In under five seconds he rapidly came up with at least one hundred potential disasters and that clock was still ticking. Images of fire, smoke, blood, and the plane falling from the sky ...

Go to sleep the moment they boarded the plane. That was the only way he would survive. He wasn't the least bit tired but he could fake it. Besides, surely, on a flight this long she would fall asleep.

The hands he had shoved into his pockets to keep from yanking out his hair now came out and laid at his sides. This would be a piece of cake.

"Is everything okay?" she asked.

"I just remembered some business I needed to take care of."

"I hope it worked out."

"Thank you." He rubbed his palms up and down his thighs. Be cool.

Breathe in, breathe out.

In.

Out.

All this Zen breathing crap wasn't working!

"Can I get you another?"

Beth thought they would have a quick drink and then he would bolt but he was easy to talk to and - once he wasn't angry with her - he was nice. "All right, thank you."

"Extra foam?"

"That's right, and a little sweet."

Sweet. Just like her.

He should have walked away.

So much for that quick, casual drink.

Aidan returned with two whiskey sours and handed Beth hers before sitting down with his own.

"Sláinte." He caught himself before actually clinking his glass with hers. He didn't need to invite another accident and he didn't have another change of clothes.

"That's how the Irish say cheers, right?"

"Yes."

"I read that in a book." She drank again from her glass that was nearly empty. "That bartender makes a great whiskey sour. I don't usually drink like this but it's so good."

"I had to taste this extraordinary drink for myself." He sipped and nodded with approval. "I think our bartender has a crush on you."

"Why?"

"Because he thought we were a couple and when I told him otherwise, he looked a little too eager."

Beth smiled. "Isn't funny how people can be so presumptuous?"

Yes, they could. Anyway … "So will this be your first time going to Ireland?"

"Yes."

"You said you're going for pleasure but you don't look very excited."

"I know. I should be as excited as a puppy with two tails, right? But I'm scared I might have screwed the pooch this time."

He accidentally chuckled a little at her play on phrases. "Why is that?" *Why? Why?* Did he really need to know *why*?

Here's a why: why was she so easy to talk to? Why was he asking her these personal questions?

He knew why.

"I've haven't been out of the country in ten years. Except to Canada twice. I almost didn't renew my passport but Gram told me I should. I haven't even been on a plane."

"Ever?"

"No, I've flown but not in a while."

"Are you taking a bus tour? Meeting some friends?" He gulped with very real dread. The determination behind her eyes was unmistakable.

"No, I'm alone, I rented a car, and plan on driving around and seeing the sights for myself."

Dear God in heaven no. Bethany Spinner was going to be loose.

In Ireland.

With a car.

Unsupervised.

Did she even know they drove on the left? This was too much.

Aidan finished his drink in one gulp. "How long do you plan on being there?"

"I didn't get a return ticket yet. I have a list of places I want to see but Lauren said she wouldn't let me come home until I've traveled around for at least a month."

What did Lauren have against the Irish? What had they done to deserve this natural disaster driving around?

A month!

A whole month?

His head was spinning again.

"Aidan? You don't look so good. How do you feel?"

"You know, I think I'm tired. I'm going to put my feet up and close my eyes."

"Okay, I'll make sure you wake up in time for our flight."

He was afraid of that. "Thank you." He pushed back on his armrests and a kickstand appeared underneath his calves. Then he crossed his arms over his chest, closed his eyes, and wishing he carried rosary beads, prayed for a coma.

CHAPTER
Nine

AIDAN HAD NO SOONER CLOSED his eyes than fallen asleep. Beth observed his chest rise and fall in deep breaths. He must have been tired which wasn't surprising, considering how pale he looked. Surely, a brief nap would do him good.

Beth turned her attention back to the window. Outside the sun was shining but in the distance were rain clouds. It would probably rain by nighttime. A shiver ran up her arm. Holding an ice-cold drink was making her cold. Good thing Lauren had suggested she bring a shawl. She pushed back on her armrests and a kickstand appeared.

Beth giggled a little as she snuggled herself down and stared out the window at the air traffic control men. Some were driving around in carts, others waving orders to an incoming plane. Jeez Louise that plane was big! She tried not to think about it. A distraction was needed so she reached for her purse and rummaged inside for her phone and earbuds. Her belongings had been jumbled around when she dumped everything out at the check-in desk. She found her phone first and pulled it out, then reached back inside looking for the earbuds when her fingers touched a thick paper. She grabbed hold and pulled out a lavender envelope.

Beth tore it open and unfolded a letter from Lauren.

Dear Klutzy,

By now you have probably dropped your purse all over the floor and found this letter. Hopefully you aren't actually reading it at the check-in desk. I wanted to remind you how brave you are, and how proud I am of you for taking this trip. Gram was right, you've been living for her long enough. It's time to live for yourself and you're not allowed back here until you've had an adventure! I'll only be a phone call away and expect a call every day. If you don't, I'll worry that you've fallen into another grave or over a cliff. Wave hello to the fairies for me!

Love,

Gutsy

P.S. Find a hot Irish guy and rip his clothes off.

As Beth read the letter, tears slipped down her cheeks and her nose ran. Great. The tears she'd bottled up were now every-where and uncontrollable.

Aidan listened from his pretended sleep. Dammit. Beth was crying. Perhaps maybe she was trying not to sneeze? No, she was definitely crying.

Nope, nope, nope! No more damsels in distress! Not now, not again. Never.

Aidan didn't care how many tears she cried. He would ignore them.

She quietly sniffled again, and again.

He opened his eyes in time to see Beth wipe her eyes with her shawl. "Beth? What's wrong?"

Thwap! A startled Beth flung her hands in the air and smacked Aidan square in the face. "Did I hurt you? I'm sorry!"

Aidan rubbed his face. Thankfully she didn't have long fingernails or he might be blind. "I'll be fine," he said from under his hand. Yeah, that hurt. "Why are you crying?"

"I miss Lauren. She left me this letter and it made me homesick."

"Who's Lauren?" Why was he asking who Lauren was? He chalked it up to the age old saying, 'if you can't beat them join them.' It couldn't possibly be because she was endearing and although chatty, very warm and upbeat. Humph. He kicked that notion to the curb where it belonged. "Why don't you call her now?"

"I can't. She's in a meeting with her son's school."

She was this upset over a lousy letter? He lowered his hands from his sore nose and looked at Beth. Her beautiful complexion was now blotchy and tear-stained and her lip trembled. He reached into his bag and pulled out a small packet of tissues and offered them to her. After Beth took and used half the package she settled down. "How long has it been since you saw Lauren?"

"She drove me to the airport."

For Heaven's sake. Women. "Oh, well, that is a long time," he said with a touch more sarcasm than he'd intended.

"I won't see her again for weeks!" Beth wailed, her tears flowing again.

"You're right. I'm sorry. I shouldn't have teased you."

"She's like my sister. I miss her already and …" she looked at her watch and hiccupped, "it's only been a couple of hours!"

Big uh oh! Beth appeared to be on the verge of blubbering.

Think fast man! "What would Lauren say if she were here right now?"

Beth stopped crying and thought. "She'd yell, "Save your tears for your pillow!" She would say it to make me laugh."

"You are laughing." She hadn't noticed that she'd laughed. This was working! "What else would Lauren say?"

"She would say she's proud of me, and to get over myself and go have an adventure for once!" Beth bucked up.

"Lauren sounds like a wise woman." He'd almost said "that's my girl" but bit his tongue before it got away from him. *That's my girl? What are you thinking? She's just another damsel in distress! A pretty face. Eyes forward and keep moving.*

Aidan quickly stood up like someone had just jabbed him in the ass. "How about I get you some water and something to eat?"

Beth smiled up at him. "Thanks, but I can do that for myself."

"No, no. I can't let you do that. You stay here and dry your eyes."

"Thank you."

"Ask not what your country can do for you but what you can do for your country," Aidan muttered under his breath. His kindness wasn't all for Beth. One didn't need to be psychic to foresee how that would turn out: Beth, with her eyes filled with tears, not noticing everything around her, carrying a drink, and food. Possibly something hot …

The inevitable casualties were too much to think about.

When Aidan reappeared he carried with him a tray of cookies, fruits, and two blueberry muffins. Everything else on the buffet looked too dangerous. She could poke her eye out, or his, with a baby carrot, get third degree burns from the soup, and don't even get him started on the cubes of cheese on toothpicks. He placed the tray on the round table, then sat back down.

Beth drank from the cool bottle of water as she sighed and looked out the window. Let's see, so far she had nearly broken Aidan's foot, and his nose, ruined his shirt, cried—no bawled—like a child over being homesick, and now that guy was bringing her snacks? This adventure was off to a bang-up start.

Aidan looked at his watch. The boarding call would be soon.

Clumsy, sweet, beautiful Beth was rapidly becoming a dilemma he hadn't seen coming and he wasn't sure what bothered him more: that he was stuck with her or that deep down, he didn't mind.

CHAPTER
Ten

AIDAN PAUSED inside the plane's entryway and from between the green curtains, observed Beth staring out the window from her seat. Her red hair sparkled in the sunlight streaming in, her skin glowed. She looked harmless—but he knew better. Behind that charming innocence was a hellcat-haired catastrophe.

In other words: exactly his type.

Damn. Damn. Damn.

He was so taken with cursing himself and any fates that played a part in this travesty that he didn't notice who was standing beside her until he heard the voice offering her a glass of champagne. It was then that Beth turned in his direction. She looked terrified. But when her wide eyes found his, they smiled in warm welcome and said, "Am I happy to see you!"

And damn, again.

His heart, what was left of it, went out to her. He really wished it wouldn't. He didn't need this nonsense. His heart couldn't take being broken again.

"It's good to see you again, Aidan."

Aidan didn't have to look at the face to know who was addressing him. It was the tight-faced, bleached-blonde, helmet-haired stewardess who could never take a hint and had yet to figure out the purpose of buttons. "Would you bring me a whiskey with ice?" Aidan had yet to take his eyes off the terrified Beth. "And keep them coming." Since the good Lord had no intention of intervening with that small coma he'd prayed for, perhaps, with any luck, he could bring that coma on himself.

Then, Beth beamed her smile at him and his heart clenched.

The quicker the better!

Aidan pulled his shoulders back and headed toward his fate: the only empty seat. The other passengers were already seated and comfortable, most with a drink in one hand and an e-reader in the other. "I guess this is me," he said as he placed his carry-on in the overhead compartment.

"I can't believe our seats are beside each other. How ironic!"

"It's ironic all right." He slid down into his seat and took a deep breath through his nose.

Surely, God hated him. Beth even smelled sweet for pity's sake. How was he supposed to concentrate on not concentrating on her when she smelled better than a bakery on a Sunday morning?

As if helmet-hair heard his thoughts, she asked Beth what perfume she wore as she served Beth her champagne and Aidan his whiskey. As usual, her blouse had too many open buttons, her mouth had too much lipstick, and her hands didn't keep to themselves. Currently the one not holding his whiskey was skating up his thigh.

"I don't wear perfume," Beth said. She had been told before that she smelled nice but never knew why. Besides, never mind her scent. Flight attendants sure were friendly these days. They not only served drinks but a massage as well. Although she tried to ignore it, Beth couldn't help but see the red fingernails moving up Aidan's thigh, or the alarm in his eyes.

Suddenly Aidan had an idea. He reached over, took Beth's free hand, and in the most sickening lovey-dovey voice said, "I'm always saying my Cupcake should sweat into bottles."

Baffled, Beth blinked from over the rim of her glass.

Helmet-hair took her hand back, unhinged his tray and plunked his drink on it. "I didn't know you were married."

"Huh?" Beth asked from inside her glass.

"I always thought you were single. Except for that—"

"It's still new and we have time don't we, Cupcake?"

"What?" Beth sputtered.

Aidan widened his eyes, pleading for her to play along. Beth nodded, with a toothy, unsure smile.

"Well, how nice for you." She'd practically spit the words. The stewardess spun on her heel with her bent-out-of-shape nose in the air.

"What are you doing?" Beth asked.

"That stewardess is so dumb, she would buy reincarnation insurance."

"Aidan!" Beth burst into giggles and covered her mouth. "I think we're supposed to call them flight attendants now."

"Not her. She can be a little too attentive if you know what I mean. That woman is a—"

"I can see what she is." Beth could also see she wore a black lace bra.

"I've made this flight a dozen times and I see her almost every time. Last time, she had her fingers tangled in my hair and stroked my beard!"

Beth laughed.

"It's not funny!"

But it was! "I see, so you think if she believes we're a couple that she will leave you and your beard alone?"

"Exactly. Please? You did drop your suitcase on my foot."

Of course, Beth would play along. It's the least she could do. "Okay, but I want a better nickname than Cupcake. A good nickname should be something more personal."

He thought for a moment. More personal … Brown eyes, Angel …

That's enough of that sort of talk!

"Spinner." There. Now she sounded more like a buddy than the stranger he wished he'd met before his heart had been broken.

"What should my nickname for you be?" She deliberately listed off mushy names. "Snookums, Truffles, Honey …"

"I don't need a nickname," he said flatly while giving her the side eye.

"Spoil-sport." Aidan lifted his drink to his lips and a drop fell from the bottom of his glass. The stewardess had spilled his drink. Helmet-hair walked past and Beth hailed her down. "Excuse me, my Sweetums could use a napkin. Would you mind?"

"I don't need a napkin."

If Beth was going along with this scheme, then she was going to have a little fun. "Now somebody has a grouchy face," she said as if speaking to a toddler. "Don't pay attention to him. My Sweetums is just tired. Long night and all." She grinned knowingly at helmet-hair. Two could play this game.

The blonde left to retrieve the napkin.

Aidan turned his whole body in Beth's direction. "Sweetums?"

"You know, like that gigantic monster on The Muppets. He looks scary but he's a cream puff."

"I'm not a cream puff."

"Okay, you're not a cream puff." But, like a monster, he could be mean and scary.

Satisfied, Aidan sat back in his seat.

Beth waited a beat, allowing him to enjoy his fresh drink before making her inquiry. "What was she going to say before you cut her off?"

Beth was so easy to talk to that not answering didn't occur to him. "I had a fiancé. She ran off with my best man a week before the wedding. How's that for the worst breakup story?"

"That's awful. I'm sorry."

Although she was sincere, he could tell there was something more she wasn't saying. "You have a look in your eye like you have something to say. Don't tell me you can beat that?"

"Well, no not beat it but I can relate to the humiliation." Beth wasn't expecting something so bad and he'd said it with no emotion at all. That wasn't a good sign. She reached across and gave his free hand an encouraging squeeze then sat back.

Terrific. Now Beth felt sorry for him. Now, if that didn't piss a guy off!

"Do you feel okay? Your eye is twitching," she said.

"No, no. I'm fine. That's just something that happens …" Aidan took a long swallow of his drink, let the chilled whiskey burn down his throat, then leaned back into his roomy seat and clenched his eyes closed. Nothing was so bad when you were blind drunk and he was halfway there.

Beth, who was already halfway through her second champagne, lowered her glass. "I'll be quiet and won't bother you." She stayed quiet for a few long seconds watching the other passengers pass by, looking at her spacious seat with envious eyes. Beth couldn't blame them. Between the free drinks, and heated massaging chair that, after pressing a few buttons she learned extended into a full bed, first-class was growing on her. And she got to sit beside someone she already knew was nice. This flight would be a piece of cake. "Aidan?"

He didn't open his eyes when he replied. "Spinner?"

"I'll leave you alone, but I just wanted to say thank you."

"What for?"

"Being so kind."

His heart tugged his eyelids open. He hadn't been kind. Not really. If she only knew what he'd really been thinking, she wouldn't be thanking him. And yet, here she was doing exactly that. Well, if that wasn't a kick in the keister. He looked at her face and kindly replied, "You're welcome."

"And I'm really sorry for crushing your foot and smacking you in the face." She went quiet.

"What about for spilling your drink on me?"

"I forgot about that. Sorry." She drank more of her champagne while looking out the window. Below, two men were loading the luggage onto the plane. And by loading what that really meant was they were heaving each suitcase—with the utmost care of course—onto the plane. Beth stared as each case was tossed like a bag of trash. That was, until they reached hers. One guy grabbed a hold of the red beast with both hands and swung, but the only thing that that flew through the air, with the greatest of ease, were his legs. He landed flat on his back on the pavement.

Beth quickly closed the shade over her window.

Aidan was about to close his eyes again when suddenly Beth's backbone grew back and she had an outburst. "But you startled me! I was doing just fine until you got in the way!"

"Just fine?" He leaned forward in his seat. "You're a walking disaster! I've never in my life met someone as clumsy as you! You should come with a warning label, sister!" Okay, that jag had flown out of his mouth at an alarmingly fast speed.

Beth's face burned with embarrassment and she turned her head back to the covered window.

Way to go, Aidan. You really did it this time. Want to slap a baby too while you're at it? I'm sure there's one on the plane somewhere. Beth was facing the wall like a naughty child, apologizing for things that were accidents and what had he offered in return? Sarcasm and cruelty. And now, if he wasn't mistaken, she had quickly wiped a tear from her eye. Just ignore it. She probably had an eyelash in her eye.

That must be a large eyelash because now she had the sniffles and her shoulders trembled. "Spinner, I'm sorry. I shouldn't have said that. I didn't mean it. I'm in a bad mood and taking it out on you."

She continued looking at the wall, not turning her head. "No, you're right. I am those things."

He reached down into the seat pocket before him and drew out his bag of complimentary toiletries, found a package of tissues, and offered them to her. She looked at the small peace offering and thanked him as she pulled a tissue from the plastic and wiped her eyes and blew her nose.

For a moment, peace was restored.

Then the engines fired up, sending vibrations up her legs and panic to her brain. Beth began digging at her knee through her pants. If she didn't stop, she would scratch a hole right through the fabric.

Aidan laid a hand over hers.

His hand had a mind of its own. He nearly snatched it back, but it soothed her digging so he left it there.

She looked down at his hand over hers and thought how comforting it was to have a friend beside her.

But he wasn't her friend. He was just a stranger beside her on a plane. A stranger who, when he wasn't Mr. Cranky Britches, made her laugh and offered comfort. And since she was stuck with him for the entire flight and would never see him again, she decided that temporary friendship was better than being alone. She stopped crying, but her lip still trembled. "Gram used to tease me saying I couldn't walk and chew gum at the same time. Then, one day I was walking down the sidewalk and I blew this enormous bubble the size of my face and tripped."

"Ouch."

"Yeah, I had a lot of gum stuck in my hair that day and a goose egg from the fall." She drank the last of her champagne and looked past him staring at nothing in particular as she thought back on days gone by. "Gram used to say 'Do one thing at a time and do it well.'"

"Wise words."

"She was a wise woman. She died a couple weeks ago."

"You must miss her. I'm sorry your grandmother died." Those were the magic words to turn her waterworks back on. Good going Aidan! If you keep it up, she could cry all the way to Ireland! Thinking fast, he changed the subject as he handed her more tissues. "Do you regret making this trip?" He nearly added that it wasn't too late for her to change her mind but didn't.

Beth wiped her eyes but her tears were still falling. "I don't know. All I know is I'm scared."

Aidan looked for an attendant. Unfortunately, all he found was Helmet-hair. Oh well, she could bring a warm, wet cloth just as well as the others. And now that she believed Beth was his wife, surely, she wouldn't try anything.

He was so wrong. When Helmet-hair delivered the warm

towel, she bent down low, shoving her lack of buttons in his face.

Then again, once a bimbo, always a bimbo. Aidan shifted a little in his seat as he averted his eyes and sent her on her way.

"There now." He spoke gently to Beth. "Wipe your face and dry your eyes," he said, handing the warm cloth to Beth. He needed her to stop crying. NOW. One thing he could never resist was a woman crying. She sat forward and wiped her face, breathing in the steam from the hot cloth. "How is that? Better?"

Beth nodded from under the warm cloth.

"Thanks. I needed that," she said with a sigh. She dragged the warm cloth down her face and wiped her eyes. When she was finished, Aidan held out his hand to take the cloth from her. She looked at the open hand then at his face.

He was very handsome with his bright blue eyes …

And thick dark hair …

And he had a lovely smile when he allowed it to curl his lips …

And a very sexy, although slightly unkept, beard …

Earth to Bethany! Stop staring!

She let go of the cloth and pulled her hand back. "You said you like to travel in silence. I'll leave you alone. I'll be fine now."

Satisfied, Aidan leaned back and closed his eyes.

"And Aidan?"

He opened his eyes. "Yes, Spinner?"

"Thank you for the tissues, and the warm cloth."

"You're welcome." He closed his eyes again and got comfortable as the plane positioned itself for takeoff.

Ahhh, peaceful silence at last …

It was quiet.

Too quiet.

Aidan opened his eyes and looked to his right to find Beth

trembling and gripping one armrest so hard her knuckles were white and beads of sweat had appeared on her forehead. Good grief. So much for her feeling better. At least she wasn't crying. "Are you all right?" Obviously, she was anything but all right but what else should he have said? 'Hey you look awful—more nervous than a deer in headlights.'

In reply she pursed her lips together tightly and squeezed her eyes shut.

"What's wrong?"

"Um," she breathed in through her nose and out through her mouth. In through her nose, out through her mouth. Why was there never a paper bag when she needed one? How did you get that oxygen mask down again? "Nothing. I'm fine."

He touched his hand to hers, poked her more like, and repeated his question.

She opened one eye. "I think I might be having a panic attack," she said, trying desperately not to freak out, but the now spooling engines of the plane was a terrifying noise! Just then the static-laden voice of the captain came through the loud-speaker. Beth shushed Aidan and listened as best she could. "What did he say? I couldn't understand him! I can't do this!"

The slingshot was released and the plane rumbled as it roared up the runway to take flight. The force pressed her head back into the seat. Her eyes clenched closed.

"Well, it's too late for that now!"

"So, you're scared. That's okay! What doesn't kill you makes you stronger."

"But not everyone makes it!"

"How about another drink?" Alcohol didn't seem to affect her too much. She'd already had enough to intoxicate about anyone but she was still going strong. He could barely keep up with her. They needed more booze for this woman STAT.

"Good idea." Beth took his whiskey right from his hand and threw it back— ice cubes and all with the greatest of ease. Then as the plane lifted off the tarmac she gasped. "Oh no!"

"What?"

"I forgot!"

"What?"

"Jiminy crickets!"

"Did you just say Jiminy crickets? I thought only little girls with pigtails said Jiminy crickets."

Her eyes shot darts. "I forgot to take my motion sickness pills!"

"What are you waiting for? Take them!" He could see it all now. An hour into the flight Beth would feel sick and before making it to the lavatory, throw up right in his lap. He watched her rummaging frantically through her purse, tossing everything out, not caring where it landed. Most of it landed on his lap. Lipstick, aspirin, passport, a book that she kept on her own lap, a small first aid kit, hand wipes, butterscotch life savers, he took one of those and popped it into his mouth. Why not have a snack during the show?

"Found them!" Beth dropped a couple pills into her palm then realized she had nothing to wash them down. There were a few drops of his whiskey and melted ice still in Aidan's glass. He shoved the glass into her hand. She threw it back then made the sign of the cross.

"You're praying?"

"What? You don't believe in God?"

"I stopped believing in a lot of things. Are you going to be sick?"

She paused, held her breath, and assessed her current state of queasiness. "I don't think so. I'll probably fall asleep soon."

"Okay, well, pull yourself together! You're going to Ireland. The land of magic, music, and maise."

"Maise? What's that?"

"It means beauty." At least he was almost sure it did. If it didn't at least it made her happy. She was smiling anyway. Beth had such a beautiful smile.

He exhaled a prayer of thanks. Maybe God—who he may or may not believe in, the jury was still out—was granting him a reprieve. Beth couldn't possibly get into trouble while asleep and everyone knew motion sickness pills made you drowsy, especially when mixed with alcohol. She would soon be neutralized. Aidan would need to reassess what he believed in. Thank you, Lord!

CHAPTER
Eleven

AIDAN'S PRAYER of thanks was swiftly rescinded when Beth did not in fact fall asleep. No, as luck would have it, the combination of alcohol and motion sickness medication was a magic potion that made Beth hyper.

Very hyper.

And chatty.

Very chatty.

She should be three sheets to the wind. She should make Sleeping Beauty look alert but nooo!

Beth flipped the window shade up and gasped in fear. That was a whole lot of empty atmosphere out there! She slammed the shade back down. Then, her fear crept back into her head. Which then sparked thoughts of imminent death and regrets. "Here I am flying across the country, and across an ocean where the plane will probably go down and I've never ridden a goat or painted a picture or gone bungee jumping or had a one-night stand. I haven't ever seen a meteor shower or The Grand Canyon!"

She hadn't even taken a breath. That was impressive.

God preserve us.

So much for her promise of leaving him in peace. What we have here is a failure to communicate.

Aidan shook his head and groaned.

I am slowly going crazy, 1,2,3,4,5,6 switch. Slowly going, am I crazy? 1,2,3,4,5,6 switch.

"You know, you're awfully grumpy. Why is that?" she demanded.

Without missing a beat, he fired back. "You're awfully klutzy. Why is that?"

She laughed. "That's the nickname Lauren has for me. We call ourselves Klutzy and Gutsy."

Aidan cocked a grin. Good nicknames.

Suddenly things were going fuzzy and Aidan's face stretched from side to side. "Are we moving sideways?" Beth asked.

"No, I think you had better close your eyes."

She laid back and closed her eyes, then her eyelids flew open again and she sat up, but left her head dangling from her shoulders back on the pillow. "Why should I do what you say?" Her eyes flared but softened when she looked at him.

Jesus, Beth could talk a dog off a meat wagon. How do you turn her off? "Because, because I'm the one who's going to be your neighbor for the night and I would like some peace and quiet." He didn't mean that. The more she rambled the more he wanted to hear and the more he heard the more he wanted …

Damn it all to hell and back! And her! No! No! No!

The mishy-mushy chatter of the husband and wife sitting across the aisle interrupted Aidan's mental lashing. The wife, who was very pregnant, kissed her husband on the cheek as she stood and waved goodbye all cutesy-like before waddling off to use the bathroom. That was a bit much.

Beth lowered her voice and leaned close to Aidan. "I bet they're the type of couple that makes you ring the doorbell and say hi to the baby."

Aidan leaned in too and spoke in a hushed tone. "You've had experience with this?"

"Yes, unfortunately."

"You didn't say that with enough repulsion."

"What does that mean?"

"It means you're not grossed out, you're jealous. You want to be the one telling people to ring the doorbell. You want the station wagon, the picket fence, the pooky face, and everything."

"I know," she whined. "And I know that's old fashioned. But so, what if I do? Is that really so awful?"

He couldn't argue with her. Not about this. "No, no it's not awful at all."

They both sat back in their seats.

The blonde steward—ahem, flight attendant—with the legs up to her neck and her breasts jacked so high it wasn't entirely clear if she actually did in fact have a neck, bent down to pick up something from the floor. There was that stark view of black lace again.

Aidan looked away but caught a flicker of something in Beth's eyes. He turned back to the stewar—flight attendant—who was now standing. Then looked back at Beth staring at the map on her TV screen. He didn't bother looking to see their location. He knew they had a long, long way left to go. But why not have a little fun along the journey? If he wasn't mistaken Bethany Spinner had a mischievous streak running through all that cotton candy softness.

Aidan nudged Beth's elbow that propped up her chin. Beth

turned and looked at him. He had a troublemaking twinkle in his eye as she asked, "What? Why are you looking at me like that?"

He had intended to stir up a little mischief but Beth started clawing at her knee again. He couldn't encourage her to drink anymore, not without possibly killing her. But she would climb the walls soon if she didn't settle down. "How about some food? Maybe some fruit and cheese?" Dinner wouldn't be served for some time but Beth needed something to do with her hands other than dig a hole in her jeans.

"Can we do that?" Yes, this first-class flying was definitely the way to go.

He had already pressed his call button and helmet-hair was on her way. His snap reaction was panic but Beth swooped in playing the role of his one and only, holding his hand and after her appetizer was served, feeding her Sweetums a grape.

Aidan smiled as her fingertips grazed his chin. He could get used to this arrangement. Helmet-hair was definitely buying it, but she was giving him the stink eye. That was a nice bonus!

After she left them, and Beth was settled he asked, "What do you think of her?" He covertly pointed his finger at the blonde who was currently serving a glass of wine three rows ahead of them. She turned and glared at Aidan as she walked away.

"She's fine."

That hadn't sounded the least bit antagonistic! Things were about to get interesting. "I think you can do better than 'fine'. Come on." He waited a beat, staring Beth down with his troublemaking eyes, until he saw a spark in hers, and if he wasn't mistaken, the corner of Beth's mouth twitched. All she needed was a little nudge. "I'll start. I bet if you slapped her hair, your hand would break."

"You're so bad!"

"Come on. You don't agree?"

"Maybe."

"Come on, Spinner. Let it rip. There's nobody listening but me."

"Her skirt could be a size larger and if she pulls her face any tighter her ears will touch in the back of her head." The flight atten—nope. This broad was definitely a stewardess—walked past them again and dropped something on the floor beside another male passenger that she of course had to bend over to get. "Does she know how buttons work? She's trying too hard. Is there any part of her that isn't plastic? She must have to unscrew her jaw every night. But still, men check her out."

"I doubt that."

"You did."

"No, I—okay, maybe but that was only for not even a second." Beth had misinterpreted his look towards the blonde for affection. Wait, Beth had noticed him looking at helmet-hair? He hadn't expected that.

"She looks like Nightmare on Harlot Street. I bet she plays the violin with her teeth."

Now the flood gates were open! Aidan's mouth dropped open as his outburst of laughter erupted. Sweet Bethany had quite a delightful attitude when she was lit.

But Beth sounded jealous.

What did she have to be jealous about? Aidan wasn't hers. He wasn't even a friend, he was barely an acquaintance. Bethany Spinner, jealous? Whatever.

"Did I shock you?" she asked.

"A little," he said with a grin. "But I like this side of you." He really liked this side of her!

. . .

Aidan had a great smile when he let it split his face. A smile Beth was sure she had seen somewhere before. "You know, you look familiar. Have we met before?"

"No." He wouldn't have forgotten her.

She looked at him for another minute. There was definitely something about him. "Are you from Minnesota?"

"No, I'm not."

"I didn't think so. You don't sound like us."

He grinned. No, he didn't sound like her. Even her voice was adorable. "I moved there about a year ago. I came on an ice fishing trip with some friends and liked the place so much that I moved there."

Beth offered to share her food with Aidan and he accepted, taking an orange slice. As she placed a slice of Irish cheddar on a cracker she asked, "You said you were in a bad mood. Is that my fault?"

"No. It's something else."

Something he didn't care to talk about, obviously, or he would have said what that something was. But Beth was desperate for a distraction and since she had told him her story, crushed his foot and soaked his shirt she sort of figured they were old friends by now. So, she continued asking questions.

"Are you going to Ireland for fun?"

He'd already told her about his sister but since she was scared witless he would overlook it. He leaned over, took a slice of cheese and a cracker and settled in for a chat. "My sister is getting married."

"How nice!"

"Not exactly. This will be husband number four."

Cripes! His sister will have had four husbands and Beth couldn't find even one! "You don't like her fiancé?"

"I've never met him but I doubt he's any different from the

others. She hasn't got the sense God gave a goose." Aidan spotted the flight attendant that wasn't Helmet-hair and gestured to his empty glass, asking for another.

"Four husbands … Know what?"

Whether it was Beth's drunken talking or his drunken listening, either way Aidan had a feeling this was going to be amusing.

"Behind my back people call me Bethany Spinster. Know why? Because no man wants me." Aidan's fresh drink arrived, delivered quietly and without any fuss by a short brunette. "I don't know why. I'm nice and I'm cute enough, right?"

Aidan didn't reply, only drank. Not because he didn't agree but because he recognized a hornet's nest when he saw one.

"Although, the last guy I dated asked me to lose weight."

Aidan's blood pressure rose at the thought of Beth being treated so badly. As the Irish would say, what a feckin' eejit!

"Maybe I am a little thick in the middle—one time, I went on a diet and nearly crashed my car through a McDonald's. Rice cakes just aren't for me—but what's wrong with that? Nobody wants to hold onto a little stick figure, anyway. I mean I'm no Cindy Crawford—"

Aidan put down his glass. "Cindy Crawford?"

"Hey, she still looks hot."

He couldn't disagree with that.

"One time Lauren and I went to a spa. You know, a fat farm only with a fancy name? They fed us rabbit food, made us meditate and every day we took an 'invigorating' walk through nature."

"Was it more like running through the woods starving with your pants on fire?"

"Exactly! I wanted to die before that week was over. I don't get it. A criminal who lies, cheats, and steals is forgiven everything but if you're carrying a few extra pounds, you may as well be run out of the country on the first barge leaving port." Beth shoved a whole cracker with cheese in her mouth, chewed and swallowed. "Gram used to say the Lord asks many things of us. He does not require calorie counting."

Aidan had to admit that Gram sounded like an interesting woman.

"People are so superficial. When it's all said and done, all life is about is how we lived, how we treated others. Were you kind? Were you helpful?"

He couldn't disagree with that. Kind and helpful had once been words used to describe him but not anymore. That was troublesome.

With the food now gone, Beth laid her head back and went quiet. Long enough that he assumed her rant was done and she would soon be asleep. Which meant he would be left alone with his self-loathing. Now, there was a scary thought.

CHAPTER
Twelve

NOPE! Wrong again. Aidan was beginning to see a pattern here.

Beth fired up once again and came straight out of left field.

"What's with all the stupid abbreviations? Doesn't anyone speak normally anymore? Use your words! Why should I give any of my time to a man who can't even buy a vowel? And don't get me started on that eggplant thingy."

"Emoji's."

"Those! And since when did sending a picture of your privates translate to 'you're my one and only?' Whatever happened to sending flowers? When did sending a dirty picture become the language of love?"

"People don't care about love anymore. They confuse love with sex. They only care about sex."

Beth paused a moment and lost her train of thought. "Where was I?"

Aidan propped his chin on his fist, settling in. "Eggplants."

No, that wasn't it, was it? Things were turning foggy in her brain. "You know, I'm probably going to be a spinster my whole life. I should start getting cats. I can be the crazy cat lady and I'll keep living and the cats will keep dying and then I'll get those little paw print things in the clay the vet gives you and then have a wall—no, a whole room of pet paw prints because I keep living and they keep dying and nobody wants me and I can't have just one cat. Oh, good gracious, no! We—"

We? How many of her were in there?

"… must have at least four. Maybe even six! And if you got six why not ten? And after that why not a baker's dozen?"

"You've given this a lot of thought, haven't you?"

She took a long breath and slowed down. "I guess so. I didn't know I thought those things." Beth was drunk all right. She wasn't slurring but her thoughts and words had loosened up. "I should know better by now. But I don't. Know why?" Beth waited for Aidan to shake his head before continuing. "Because I trust people. Well, not anymore! You're looking at a newly reformed trustee." No, that wasn't the word. "Trusteder? Truster?"

"Maybe you should try kissing a frog."

"Don't think I haven't considered it," she said with a giggle. Although she hadn't given up hope of finding her Prince Charming, she was thirty-seven and had dated every eligible bachelor, and that one time by accident one not so eligible, in town. She would have to move to frogs. Pfft, and even if she found a nice guy, he probably wouldn't want her. She was always being accused of being too nice. "Aidan, why do men seem to want the mean girls?"

That was a rhetorical question. Beth was clearly on a tangent.

"I don't understand it. Why would I want to manipulate the man I share a profound connection with?"

Beth thought being in love meant having a profound connection with someone. Aidan had believed that once upon a time too ...

She looked away to the couple across the aisle. They were holding hands and watching two different movies. "You know, the kind of love that can't always be explained but you love each other just because." She looked back at Aidan, meeting his eyes. "Is there something wrong with that?"

Aidan practically sighed like a girl swooning over Elvis Presley. "No. No there isn't." His eyes drifted to the closed window shade. He looked at the time on his watch. The sun would be setting. "Mind if I open the shade?"

Although the thought made her nervous, Beth nodded her head.

Aidan couldn't have been more pleased. Outside, the setting sun illuminated the billowing clouds with brilliant shades of orange, purple and pink.

Calm now and unafraid, Beth stared out the window, hypnotized by the brilliant display of nature. Then she looked back at Aidan, who was leaning forward and stared into his eyes for a leisurely moment. Just stared. There was something about him ... What she didn't notice was him staring back.

Then Beth blinked, breaking the spell, and flipped her hand, accidentally whacking Aidan's forearm. "It's okay. I don't need a boyfriend, or a husband to make me happy. But it would be nice maybe to find a nice guy." She'd used the word nice too much but no matter how hard she concentrated, she couldn't come up with another word.

"One of those rare good ones?"

She nodded. "You wouldn't happen to know one, would you?"

"I used to know one but he's not around anymore." That was about enough of that. New topic please!

Since Beth showed no sign of stopping and Aidan desperately wanted to change the subject, he suggested they play one of the onboard games. That was innocent enough and a simple, friendly game would pass the time.

After an hour of playing not so simple and friendly trivia, Aidan had lost every round, except one. He hadn't let her win. He didn't need to. As it turned out, Beth was a smart cookie. She was also a closet ruthless cutthroat who was so immersed in the game that when the announcement about turbulence ahead came, she hadn't worried for a moment.

"I've got bad news, Sweetums. Your walking Tupperware party of a girlfriend died of humiliation watching you lose to me."

"You know, you're awfully competitive!"

"You're observant. Now, are you going to play or do you want to do each other's nails instead?"

Oh, baby. Having their seatbelts on during turbulence turned out to be crucial. Not because of the plane shaking but because he felt the urge to dive across the seat and kiss her.

Stop it!

CHAPTER
Thirteen

BETH EMERGED from the bathroom with her shirt splotchy and wet, her hair disheveled, and her eyes red. All that was missing was blood and maybe a few bruises. Exactly how could she have gone into the bathroom looking perfect and come out looking like she had gone a round with a fire hose? Aidan couldn't help but ask.

Beth started by describing having to be a contortionist just to close the bathroom door, then she stubbed her toe when she lifted the lid to the toilet—the loud sucking noise startled her—then she tripped when getting her pants pulled up, and—

"And the dish ran away with the spoon."

"Then that foamy soap splattered all over my shirt when I washed my hands so I washed it off."

"And then you ended up looking like you flushed yourself down the toilet."

Beth nodded. "I had a brief conversation with your girlfriend too."

Oh brother. "Go on."

"First of all, her name is Viki spelled with a K."

"I don't care." She could be the Queen of the Nile and he wouldn't care.

"Anyway, she's been watching us and thinks you are quite the romantic."

Aidan stared, uninterested.

"She also said we make a perfect couple and hopes we have a happy life together. I thought she might melt into a puddle at my feet."

"If only she could."

"I would probably slip in it. I'm a little clumsy."

"Really? I hadn't noticed." Aidan winked with a smile. "Come on, let's hear it. What's the worst clumsy thing you ever did as a nurse?"

She didn't need to think about this one. "I tripped and broke my nose on a patient's walker then they slipped in the blood gushing out of my nose and broke a hip, which then caused them to have a heart attack, then they went into a coma, lived for three days and died."

He sat. Motionless. Staring. His lips only slightly apart for what seemed like forever. Beth was kidding right? She had to be kidding. He blinked hard and burst into laughter. "You're funny."

"The first part was true."

"What?"

She looked at him with guilty eyes. "I really did trip. I don't even know on what. My own two feet I guess, and I broke my nose on a patient's walker and he slipped but the rest was made up. He was fine except for a couple of bruises and being in dire need of a bath."

Again, without Aidan's consent his hand laid on hers, patting it. "That could happen to anyone." Be serious. No, no it couldn't. They shared a sideways look and laughed together. "So, you didn't only take care of your grandmother?"

"No, she didn't need full time care until a couple of years ago. I had other nursing jobs."

"What will you do now?"

"I don't know. I guess I wanted every moment I could get with Gram. I never thought about what was next."

A tear escaped from the corner of Aidan's eye and he quickly wiped it away. "Well, I can't blame you for that." Again, his hand was patting hers. Seriously? Come on!

"What's the clumsiest thing you ever did?" she asked.

"When I was, I think eight years old, I swung the kitchen door the wrong way causing my mother to splat an entire sheet cake onto herself."

"I've done that. Rookie."

"Okay Spinner, then what's the clumsiest thing you've ever done of all time?"

That was an easy answer. "I fell in a grave."

"What?" Aidan couldn't believe what was coming out of his mouth but there they were. "I think I need to hear this story. An open grave?"

Beth nodded her head long and slow, staring at her lap and recalling that event in the not-so-distant past. "Yep. I fell six feet down into an open grave." She recalled Lauren shoving Danny then looked at Aidan with a smile in her eyes. "Luckily nobody was in it." She gestured her hand into a swan dive. "The guy I was dating, Danny, dumped me at Gram's funeral and I was so upset that I backed away from him and …"

"You fell into a grave. That's somehow so much worse than the broken nose story. Did the guy help you out?"

"No," she said shaking her head and looking away as if down into the grave. "Lauren did. She's my best friend."

"Yes, you've mentioned her."

"Oh, that's right. She heard me shriek when I fell and came running. Then after she got me out, Lauren pushed Danny in, and we walked away arm in arm with him screaming like a baby in the distance." Beth twiddled her fingers as if running away toward the window.

"That's a perfect ending to that story." Aidan held up his whiskey and said, "To good friends."

"It is, isn't it? That's how most of my stories with Lauren are. She and I have been friends since kindergarten."

"We really can pick them. I marry a woman who's sleeping with somebody else and you date juvenile minded grave dumpers."

"Yep," she said with a popping P. "So, what do unlucky people like us do?"

Aidan held up his glass before taking a sip. He'd lost count of how many drinks he'd had. He was somewhere between feeling no pain but not yet seeing double. All in all, it was a peachy place to be. "I drink and write bad books."

"You're an author?"

Aidan nodded and took a bite of his herb roasted potatoes. "Though, not a very good one. Not anymore anyways."

"So, you're in a slump. You'll find your way out."

Beth said it with such ease and goodwill that he believed her. Yes, he was as she put it "in a slump" but he'd written good books. Really good books.

"I love to read." She thought for a moment. "I don't remember reading any of your books. Now that I've met you though, I will. What is it you write?"

"Hold on to your hat but I write romantic fiction."

Beth raised a forkful of beef to her mouth but her hand froze in mid-air. Romantic fiction? This guy? She thought he would say crime thriller or something. Because she was now stumped on what to say she took her bite.

Who knew telling Beth what his job was would be the thing to make her stop talking? Except that now, he was used to the sound of her voice and as much as he hated to admit it, missed the conversation. "I know, it's surprising that someone as cynical as me writes romance."

"I don't think you're cynical, not really. I think you're sad and you express your grief with sarcasm."

He tried not to look like she had smacked him between the eyes. "What makes you think I'm sad?"

"I don't know exactly. You feel a little sad to me is all."

"You're just saying that because I told you about my fiancé."

"That's not it. I can't really say why. You just seem sad. Not heartbroken though."

If she could "feel" his sadness then what else could she sense about him? She wasn't wrong. "As it happens, I suppose I am. My last two books have been rejected. The last one was rejected this morning. That's why I was less than forgiving when you ran into me. Sorry."

"That's okay. Everyone has bad days and you weren't that mean about it."

"Yes, I was."

"But I yelled at you."

"You call that feeble attempt at a tirade yelling?" It had been like more like being told off by a kitten.

"Are you saying I can't stick up for myself?"

"No, I'm saying that what you were doing wasn't yelling." She could yell at him any day of the week. "Next time give it a little more oomph."

She didn't know if she was capable of oomph when it came down to defending herself but she would try. Then, another thought came. "Do you know Kate Connolly? She's my favorite author."

He choked a little on his food and coughed, then drank some water before replying, "Our paths have crossed."

"What's she like?"

"She can be prickly but once you get to know her, she's nice."

"Kate wrote my favorite book. I've read it dozens of times and I always have a copy with me." She reached into her personal shelf and brought out her paperback. When she retrieved the book, it was upside down, displaying the back cover featuring a picture of the author. She had a smile like Aidan's. Beth examined the picture for a moment. "You know you look a lot like her. Maybe that's why I thought we'd met before." The more Beth looked at the picture and then at Aidan the more the similarities showed. It was uncanny.

Aidan admired the tattered cover with its picture of the Irish countryside and for the briefest of moments smiled. But that didn't last long. The cynic had to have his say and he needed to divert her attention from that picture. "I'm familiar with that story. So, what, you think that because it happened in a novel that you will go to Ireland and have a serendipitous run-in with your one true love? I've got news for you Spinner, that only happens in novels."

"No, of course I don't think that. The idea of going to Ireland came from my love of the book but I'm not going to find a boyfriend."

"Then why are you going?"

"It was Gram's dying wish." She reached into her purse again and pulled out Gram's letter.

Aidan wiped his hands on his cloth napkin before taking hold of what was clearly a precious commodity. Most people didn't travel with letters but Beth traveled with two. He pulled the single sheet of daisy-embellished stationary and first admired the elegant handwriting. One didn't see cursive writing much anymore. With Beth's permission he read it aloud.

My Dear Bethany,

If you are reading this then I have returned home to your grandfather. You have been so good to me. No grandmother could have asked for a better granddaughter than you. When your parents died, I worried day and night over you. I wondered if I was doing a good job raising you, if I was doing right by you, would you resent me for not being your mother? All those nights spent worrying were a waste because you were a wonderful child. You gave up your life to take care of me. I know you don't see it that way but you missed out on some things because of me. There is one last thing I need you to do for me. I want you to take that trip to Ireland that you've been dreaming about. I want you to walk along those shores, pass through the green fields, make new friends. You never know, maybe your true love is waiting for you there just like in your favorite book. It will be scary, I know, but you're braver than you think. Thank you for staying with me, and for giving this old woman a better life than she could ask for. Now, go live yours and save your tears for something that's sad. Like Bambi. Because of you I had a wonderful life. There's nothing sad about that.

Love,
Gram
P.S. Find a handsome Irishman and rip his clothes off.

After a small chuckle at the last line, Aidan folded the letter and placed it back inside its envelope then handed it back to Beth.

"That's a beautiful letter and testament to you." He looked up and saw Beth wiping her eyes and restrained himself from moving in.

Damn it all to hell and back, Beth needed a hug.

He could hold her for just a minute, couldn't he? What could a harmless minute possibly do?

It could do exactly what it had done the last time he'd fallen victim to a woman's tears that's what it could do!

But something told him Beth was different. One only had to look into those innocent wet eyes of hers to see.

Different or not, this wasn't a good idea.

He leaned back again, thinking of what to say to the crying woman beside him. He placed his hand over hers that laid on her lap and waited for her to make eye contact before speaking. "Spinner, you can't put a price on peace of mind."

"I could've put my grandmother in a home or hired a nurse to take care of her, but I never would've forgiven myself! I wanted to take care of her! And I could. I wanted to, dammit! Sorry. I didn't mean to swear. A lot people at the funeral kind of said I've wasted my life." Tears came again.

Oh God. Aidan's white horse reared. Down boy, down!

"I'm sorry for crying again. I don't know what's wrong with me."

"You still have time. How old are you?"

That snapped her out of her crying jag. "That's rude."

"Well, I thought you didn't regret taking care of your grandmother?"

"I didn't! I don't!" she said a little too loudly.

"It doesn't sound like that to me."

"All I meant was, I'm disappointed in myself for not doing more." She blew her nose, hopefully for the last time. Aidan handed her a fresh packet of tissues. "I guess I've been waiting for something to happen instead of making something happen. Does that make sense?"

"Yes."

Beth pushed back her hair from her face and smiled the soft smile that was quickly becoming irresistible. "But I'm making something happen now."

Yes, she was. And much more than she knew.

Right on her interruptive cue Viki spelled with a K brought their desserts. Aidan had a chocolate cheesecake, Beth had a fresh berry tart. Both looked delicious. And both looked as if they needed the other to be whole.

"Want to see another benefit of flying first class?" Aidan asked.

Beth nodded with excitement.

Aidan pressed his button to summon Viki.

"What can I do for you two?"

Aidan cleared his throat and sat back further in his seat in case she wasn't as thrilled for the happy couple as she'd said. "We would like another slice of cheesecake and another tart."

"Aren't they delicious? I don't blame you for getting another." Viki smiled and turned to leave but Aidan stopped her. "And two whiskies, no ice." He turned back to Beth who was practically clapping.

"That is so cool!"

Viki promptly returned with a smile and their order.

Aidan raised his whiskey up in a toast, prompting Beth to do the same. "To Gram, may she rest in peace knowing you're granting her wish."

Beth nodded, trying not to cry yet again. There had been enough tears on this flight, thank you.

They clinked their glasses and each took a drink and a respectable moment of silence.

"So, are you going to keep to your grandmother's wishes and rip off of some unsuspecting man's clothes?"

Still tipsy and happy to continue riding that train Beth replied, "Why? Are you volunteering?" then laughed. "It couldn't be you anyway if I'm sticking to what Gram wants. She said an Irishman." Her eyebrows shot up and she gasped. "Ope! I can't believe I said that!"

Aidan laughed in his throat. That wasn't the most shocking thing Beth had said but there was no need to point that out and embarrass her more than she was already.

Then again … "My mother is Irish."

The adorable blush that flooded Beth's face was worth it.

Since she now had two desserts to indulge herself with Beth thought it best to put her book away. Then she saw it. She looked from the author's picture to Aidan and back again. "Aidan?"

"Yes?" he replied taking a bite of chocolate. Then he looked at her and realized she knew or she was close to it. With a sigh he wiped his mouth with a napkin then placed it down and confessed. "That's my sister."

"Kate Connolly is your sister?"

"No, that picture is my sister but she didn't write the book. I did. I'm Kate Connolly. I use my sister's picture and a woman's name because women tend to prefer female authors."

"I knew I recognized you!" This was amazing! "Would you sign my book?"

"No."

His voice was bitter so she didn't ask again, even though she wanted to.

The way Aidan saw it, soon he would need a plunger to salvage his career. Since she who shall remain nameless left, everything he wrote was pure, unadulterated crap. At least that's how his publisher had put it. And so eloquently too. He didn't want his fiancé back, didn't miss her. He wasn't pining. But he would be lying if he didn't admit that her leaving had, shall we say, soured his outlook on relationships and in turn soured his writing. Some suggested he try writing thrillers. He didn't want to read thrillers much less write them. Maybe it was time to accept that his career as an author was finished. If anything, that upset him the most.

"That's really your favorite book?"

"I've read it so many times I know it inside out!"

"Why do you keep reading it? It's just a romance novel. Those are a dime a dozen."

"Do you like coffee?"

"Yeah why?"

"Do you have your coffee the same way every time?"

"What's your point?"

"If it's okay for you to drink coffee the same way every single day, why isn't it okay for me to want to read the same thing over and over? Besides, it's not just another romance novel. It's a book about hope, loss, and finding beauty."

"You would think you were reading *War and Peace* the way you talk about it."

"I have read War and Peace. It took me six months to finish. I read your book in a day. Listen, I'm sorry your last couple of books haven't made the cut but the woman, sorry, man who wrote this book, my favorite book, still has a lot more to offer."

"It bothers you that a man wrote it, doesn't it?"

"No, no … Pfft nooo. You have the need for privacy. I can understand that."

"So, no then?"

"Of course, it doesn't. The characters you created are who readers take into the darkness with them. When they need comfort, they choose your book, your characters to share those moments. Do you really not know how intimate that is?"

"I hadn't thought about it like that."

"Aidan, you wrote a beautiful story. When I want to laugh, I read this book. When I need to cry, I read this book. When I need to feel love, I open this book. It's all in here. You can feel the love they have for each other leap off the page. And that makes me feel loved too. The author who wrote this isn't a failure."

"You should be in charge of my promotions."

"And you should have more faith in your talents. Maybe you will find some inspiration on your visit?"

"Maybe." Doubtful but maybe. Either way he was tired of talking about himself. "How about another game, Cupcake?"

Beth smiled and put her paperback away. "You're on, Sweetums."

CHAPTER
Fourteen

THEY APPROACHED Ireland as the sun was rising. Beth had been peacefully asleep for the past hour, but Aidan couldn't resist rousing her, eager to witness the sparkle in her eyes as she glimpsed Ireland for the first time. His anticipation outweighed any consideration for her rest.

"Spinner? Wake up." Her eyes fluttered open, and she smiled softly at the sight of his face. "Look out your window." Nothing beat the view of Ireland from the sky.

Beth sat up and rubbed her eyes as she looked out the window. Then her eyes were filled the wonderous sight of the Emerald Isle at the start of a new day. "Aidan! That's Ireland down there! It's beautiful already!" Her eyes glistening with happy tears as she watched the sea crash against the rocky shores. "Are those stone walls? And look how green it all is! And look! A rainbow over there!"

Aidan worried for a moment. Over there, on the west side of the island, was where they were headed. And by the looks of the quickly graying sky the rain was barely getting started. Beth's picture of Ireland was one he'd painted for her in his book. He hoped that picture wasn't drowned by what looked like storm clouds. That was no way for her first trip to be.

Beth's face was mushed into the window as her feet danced with excitement. His anticipation was satisfied.

"So, what do you think?"

Beth turned around, her face glowing, her smile wide. "It's already even more beautiful than I thought it would be."

Aidan's lips parted as if to speak but then they closed again.

"Thank you, for waking me up."

"You're welcome."

———

Thankfully, they were first in line through customs. Aidan hated waiting in that large, dreary, dank, room and the faster he and Beth parted ways the better. All he had to do now was wait for his suitcase to appear on the luggage trolley, grab it, and go. Which wasn't going to be easy. Beth had already been run over by the crowd of passengers trampling through the airport, all of them eager to stretch their legs and breathe fresh air. Her shoelace had come untied causing her to trip and heaven forbid anyone slow down for a second. Aidan worried what would happen to her after they parted ways. Who would catch her when her shoelace came untied again? He told himself that that could have happened to anyone. That wasn't a clumsy moment therefore wouldn't repeat itself.

They made their way to the baggage claims and waited in comfortable silence as they watched case after case slide down the chute onto the carousel, each one landing with a harsh thud. Then Aidan's case appeared. He lifted it from the parade of luggage then returned to Beth's side to wait for hers.

They waited and waited.

"I guess that barge travels slower than the plane?"

Aidan barked a laugh. "They're probably hoisting your suitcase off the deck as we speak."

There was no doubt when Beth's case had finally arrived. A thunderclap echoed off the airport walls. Beth clenched one eye closed and winced.

"No, I couldn't let you do that. I can handle it." Beth positioned herself at the side of the carousel, planted her feet square with her shoulders, and waited for her case to round the corner. It approached and she got a hold of the handle but struggled to lift the case. If she could pause the moving carousel, she would have a fighting chance!

"Here, let me help you," Aidan offered.

Beth was going to get this confounded case off this trolley on her own even if it killed her! She had only another second or two before it would drag her with it so she needed to act fast.

One, two, three, HEAVE!

She pulled with all of her might and swung it from the clutches of the carousel—right into Aidan's knees.

Her case landed with a thump on the floor. Aidan's case tipped over underneath him. And Aidan landed flat on his back with his feet in the air like a dead cow.

"Aidan!"

His head was spinning. Somewhere in the blurry distance Beth's voice called to him.

Merrily, merrily, merrily, merrily. Life is but a dream.

Aidan opened his eyes and blinked Beth's face into focus. What in the hell had just happened? One minute he was going to help Beth, next thing he knew up was down and down was up and his feet were over his head! Now Beth was touching him everywhere!

"Aidan, lay still, you could have a concussion."

"I think we can aim a little higher than that." He groaned as he sat up feeling as if he'd cracked a rib. He'd gone down like a sack of hammers and was pretty sure his eyes were spinning in two different directions and who ordered the Tweety birds? Ugh, you always think it's going to happen to somebody else.

"Let me help you."

"No, no. That's all right." He pushed himself up on his elbows and waited for the flapping birds to disappear as he pressed his palm against his forehead to silence the rolling gong inside his head. "I would like to keep Ernie around."

"Ernie?"

"That's what I named my last brain cell." Clearly, he had lost every other one back in Minneapolis.

Nurse Spinner finished her assessment of his injuries. There wasn't any blood but there was a bump that was surely going to be sore. "You aren't driving, are you? You really shouldn't. I can drive you wherever you need to go."

Drive? Did she say drive? How had he forgotten that Beth was going to drive?

Here!

In Ireland!

Oh, no. Aidan sprung up from the floor. "That won't be necessary. I'm not driving and look," he moved his head from side to side and followed his own finger with his eyes, "All good. No need to worry."

Impressed by his swift recovery Beth stood up but before she could say anything he continued.

"Listen, my ride is waiting for me so I have to go." Aidan grabbed hold of his suitcase in a hurry then paused. This wasn't how he wanted to leave her but the more he thought about it the harder his head throbbed, the tighter his chest clenched, and if that didn't piss him right off! How did this, this, this, pain in the neck, intrusive, klutzy ... kind, and perfectly lovable woman manage to—

Nope. We are not going there!

He reached out and took her hand to shake it. "Good luck, Spinner. Be careful out there. Just remember to hug the middle line when you're driving, and don't worry." He made the mistake of looking into her eyes. There were so many things he wanted to say. Warnings, tips, sweet nothings ...

Dammit! Stop it! Enough already!

He picked up her red suitcase from the floor, setting it up beside her with a nod. It wasn't supposed to be hard to leave. He had resigned himself to engaging with her for the flight and then he was supposed to pick up his luggage and walk away. Then again, she did knock him flat on his backside. "You'll be fine. I hope Ireland lives up to your expectations." With that he turned and hurried away.

Beth stood and watched Aidan reach the doors where a woman rushed into his outstretched arms, throwing herself at him and plastering his face with kisses then linked her arm with his as they strode through the airport doors.

Jeez Louise! He could have mentioned having a girlfriend!

Beth's cheeks flushed with embarrassment as she waited, almost expecting he might turn around to wave a last goodbye. But he didn't. The doors closed behind the happy couple and they disappeared.

So, that was that. It wasn't like they would ever see each other again anyway. Why should he turn around? Aidan had made her flight easier and for that she was grateful.

Aidan may have been gruff at first but underneath all that was empathy and kindness. At least there had been before she swept his feet out from underneath him. Was it any wonder he'd run away?

With a sigh she lifted her suitcase from the floor. Right outside the sliding doors, the green hills and rocky shores of Ireland awaited.

CHAPTER
Fifteen

BETH SAT in the driver's seat of her rented silver hatchback, petrified as a deer caught in headlights. This was the tiniest rental car they offered, roughly the size of a matchbox, but from the left side felt like a tractor trailer.

It didn't help anything when the rain had begun when she stepped outside the airport. The man at the rental counter had been far from amiable, initially pushing a standard shift car on her and forcing her to plead for an automatic. Beth attributed his demeanor to the early hour and likely exhaustion. Working an airport rental counter couldn't be easy, after all. Never mind that she had been the one and only customer.

She plotted her course to the town of Ennis in County Clare on her GPS.

Bowling-ball sized raindrops battered the car. With the sound beating on her eardrums she couldn't think and panic gripped her throat. Then, she recalled Aidan's voice reassuring her.

Holding her breath, Beth ever so carefully backed out of the parking space, then let it out in one big shaky sigh. So far, so good. Turn left, the GPS instructed.

She could do this. One turn at a time.

The windshield wipers ran back and forth, back and forth, making an awful screeching noise even though the glass couldn't be more wet. The sound grated her nerves and with each stroke her tears burned more and more.

Save your tears for your pillow, Bethany Spinner!

She merged onto the highway, which she quickly saw they refer to as the motorway, turned right and headed towards … Waterford. She was going the wrong direction.

Welcome to Ireland.

The sunrise she had admired from the plane was now hidden by a massive rain cloud whose color she had never seen before. She was pretty sure she'd left a dent in the car when she heaved her suitcase into the trunk with all her might—and missed. At least she had gotten into the car on the correct side. But let's face it, even that was an accident.

Well, what did she expect? Rolling hills with a castle right beside the airport?

Maybe. So, what?

Piece of cake …

Easy peasy …

Nope. She called Lauren and nearly jumped when the phone call went through the car speakers. Okay! Now we know the bluetooth works in the car. Check. Lauren answered the phone on the second ring.

"Beth, hi!" Lauren said in a raspy voice.

"You sound tired."

"It's two o'clock in the morning here." In all the excitement Beth had forgotten about the time difference. "How was your flight? Lauren had been watching the clock, wringing her hands with worry. The more she thought of her best friend alone in a foreign country the more she wondered if she had made a huge mistake encouraging her to make the trip. DO YOU THINK SO?

"The flight would have been awful if it weren't for Aidan." That reminded her! "Speaking of which, you'll never believe who I ran into."

"Elvis? I heard sightings were up this month."

"Hilarious."

Suddenly Lauren didn't sound so tired. "How long do I have to wait before you tell me who Aidan is?"

"Another passenger. I ran into him." Lauren knew her friend well enough to know that when she said "ran into him" she meant it in the most literal sense. "I dropped my suitcase on his foot."

"Oh, Klutzy." Lauren shook her head. "We should have gone shopping for luggage."

"I know. Anyways, I ran into him and he wasn't very nice so I sort of yelled at him."

"You what?" Beth stuck up for herself? This was a moment for the books! "What did you yell?"

"I don't know what came over me but I told him not to be so mean."

All the times Beth had witnessed Lauren yelling at people and the best she came up with was calling him mean? Oh well, she had to start somewhere.

"Then I ran into him again and spilled my drink on him."

"Two for two! I'm proud of you!" Lauren teased.

A pair of headlights came into view in Beth's rearview mirror. Her heart stopped beating until it passed and was far away ahead. "It turned out our seats were next to each other on the plane."

Lauren's blood pressure boiled. Why couldn't the powers

that be at least give her a pleasant plane ride? Was that too much to ask? "I'm sorry."

"Why? He's great! You won't believe it! He's really Kate Connolly."

"The author? You mean Kate had a sex change?"

"No. He uses a female pen-name, bonehead." See, Beth could throw out an insult when she wanted to.

"No way! What's he like? What's he look like?"

"He looks like he's an Iron Man champion who scratches his back with a fork. And he's, I don't know, sad. Like he's crying but the tears aren't falling." Talking about Aidan, her frazzled nerves all but disappeared even though the bowling balls still pelted the car and it was darker than dark. "We didn't exchange phone numbers. He looked at me a lot like my dress was stuck in my pantyhose." The only way Beth would know that was if she had actually had her dress stuck in her pantyhose. And she had. Twice. No, three times. Then there were the few times he'd looked at her with tenderness. And laughed with her, teased her … She hated to admit it but Beth could see why that stewardess wanted him. "Besides, he has a girlfriend."

"How do you know?"

"I saw her at the airport and her chest is so big I bet she wears ankle weights under her socks to keep her from tipping over!"

"You sound jealous."

"I am not!"

"Now you're whining."

"Am not!"

"Now you're pouting."

"What is your point?"

"If I didn't know any better, I would say you have a thing for Aidan."

"I do not!"

This couldn't be a coincidence! An idea formed in Lauren's head. An idea she would keep to herself for the time being but there were questions that needed answers. She wanted to hear everything, and encouraged Beth to drive.

Beth told her about Aidan, their flight, and the stewardess. How they talked and talked and played trivia and cards. Lauren made Beth repeat that bit.

Fun fact about Bethany Spinner: although she was the nicest woman, she had a competitive streak. An ugly one.

So, Beth dropped her suitcase and spilled her drink on him, and he still played trivia, watched out for her, and talked with her for the entire flight? That idea was gradually forming. But then it fell apart when Beth said she'd hit him like a wrecking ball.

"What am I going to do with you?"

"How about not sending me to Ireland all by myself? A bolt of lightning cracked the darkness, illuminating the passing landscape. Beth lost her concentration for a moment and began veering into the other lane. Luckily, no other cars were near her. "Oh my gosh! I just passed a castle!"

"Really?"

"It was just there in the middle of a field!"

"Your first castle sighting! How exciting! Now, tell me more about Aidan." Lauren had priorities and while castle sightings were fun, they were not on the list right now.

Beth looked in her rearview mirror to try and get a glimpse of the ruins again but saw nothing but darkness. "I doubt I'll ever see Aidan again. He's only here for his sister's wedding."

If that didn't suck pickled ass …

After driving the wrong way down two one-way streets, and

backing out from both, narrowly avoiding a shop window or two, Beth finally reached the hotel.

"What will you do today? Can you walk around town?" Lauren asked.

"That's a good idea. I can walk inside the shops instead of backing through their windows. I think there's an old church here too."

"You know what Gram used to say: Life is like a dogsled team. If you're not the lead dog the scenery never changes." Lauren got out her tarot deck and shuffled.

"I'm scared."

"I know, sweetie. But I have a good feeling about this. You're meant to be there." Lauren flipped up a tarot card. "Just ask Ursula, nine of cups. She says you're meant to be there too."

If Ursula says so then it must be true.

So Beth didn't know how to get in touch with him. Maybe there was still hope. A man who could handle Beth's antics and not run away screaming was not only rare but unheard of.

The more Lauren thought about it the more she was convinced, Aidan Turner must be found.

CHAPTER
Sixteen

THE RAIN that had so generously welcomed Beth when she arrived in Ireland was still falling. It had been four long, soggy, dark days. Morning after morning, or afternoon after afternoon if she was honest, jet lag weighed her down. She might have been able to shake it if the sun appeared. But since the sun didn't seem to exist in this country her outlook became dark as the sky.

This wasn't like Beth at all. She wasn't one to wallow and sulk and yet that's precisely what she'd been doing. But in her defense, she had finally made it to Ireland and all it did was rain. She had been nowhere. She had seen nothing except nearly every season of *Murder, She Wrote* on TV. Ireland had little to offer in the digital entertainment department. She had ordered everything offered for room service—her favorite items on the menu so far were the cheesy potatoes, stuffed roast chicken, and the chocolate raspberry tart. While on her scouting expedition Beth found an elegant sitting room and from there, through the eight-foot-tall windows, she saw a garden with a gazebo. She braved the downpour to go sit outside under the protection of the gazebo. Beth stepped into the vestibule and there, asleep in a small bed was a cat curled up cute as you please. Even he had the sense to stay indoors. She looked through the doors in front of her at the river of water flowing down the glass, sighed and turned back for her room.

Enough feeling sorry for yourself!

Well, when in Rome. Or in this case, Ireland. The Irish lived with the rain just fine, so could she.

Beth got dressed, put on her jacket, and texted Lauren, thanking her for suggesting she bring her duck boots, then headed out for the street. Outside was a town, centuries old, and the ruins of a Friary she was aching to see. And according to the friendly hotel manager, it was all within walking distance. That put her at ease. If she had to drive in town again, she might have a nervous breakdown. Whether that breakdown began before or after she ran the car through a shop window was irrelevant.

Ennis was a charming market town with shops ranging from what they called a pound shop (which was a dollar store, never mind that Ireland no longer used pounds as currency. That was a little confusing,) to antique stores. She had never seen so many used violins in her life. There was a very nice jewelry store where she bought absolutely nothing. Buying something as cele-bratory as jewelry didn't seem at all appropriate. Not unless they had a magic ring that would transport her home or at least change the weather. There was even an old man playing his fiddle and singing underneath an entryway, safe from the rain, but only just. His case was open at his feet for donations. Beth reached inside her wallet and left him fifty euros. Not because he was particularly good but anyone who dared perform on a day like this needed that money more than she did.

Beth would have surely been lost if it weren't for the two

towering landmarks on either side of town: the Cathedral of Saints Peter and Paul and the Daniel O'Connell monument. She could always see one of them and all she had to do was head in that direction to find her way.

Behind a great stone wall and iron gates were the imposing, magnificent ruins of Ennis Friary. Wow. To step through centuries old halls, see the graves, admire the limestone sculptures. This was something she could never have seen back in Minnesota.

Now back in her room, shaking off her wet coat, her thinking changed. Sure, it was raining now and had been for days but the rain had to stop falling eventually, and today she proved Ireland could be enjoyed even in the lousy weather. As she combed her fingers through her long, wet curls, she decided. Tomorrow she would load up her suitcase and travel to a new location. A bed and breakfast would be a pleasant change of scenery. Maybe she could find one near the sea somewhere along what was called the Wild Atlantic Way. It was supposed to be a can't-miss route.

Besides, happiness can be acclimated, right?

She would be fine.

This would be fun!

Look out Wild Atlantic Way, here comes Bethany Spinner!

CHAPTER
Seventeen

FOUR MORE DAYS and four bed and breakfasts later …

Beth wasn't one for curses but she dearly hoped that hotel manager contracted a flesh-eating bacteria. The Wild Atlantic Way was the worst route on earth!

Beth was being punished. She didn't know what for but this was no vacation, this was no adventure, this was torture, and if she had to stay another day on this soggy God-forsaken island it would be a hostage situation!

Beth wanted to go home. Ireland had chewed her up and spit her out. There was no romance here. No beauty. She had gone to the cliffs of Moher only to get blown over by the wind into the ever-present mud. She visited a stud farm where a horse stomped on her foot, causing her to fall into a pile of manure. She got lost somewhere in the mountains on what one local called a shortcut with only sheep to turn to for help. And beside the hotel, each place she stayed had a shower smaller than a shoebox, no hot water, no heat, and if she was served smoked salmon one more time, she was going to lose what little sanity she had left!

All in all, Ireland was a shamrock-shaped wad of disappointment and regret.

Her clothes caked in manure would need to be placed in a plastic bag because heaven forbid there be a laundromat! She furiously wadded up her clothes and shoved them into her suitcase directly on top of her favorite book. If her book got dirty, oh well! All the stories about the "breathtaking" landscape, the "kindness of the Irish," the "magic that danced on the air." Aidan, Kate, whoever he was, made it all up! If he was with her right now, she just might slap him!

With that thought she slammed the lid and locked it shut.

She didn't know how far away the airport was but it didn't matter. She wasn't spending another night here.

Beth heaved her suitcase down two flights of stairs, dragged it through the rain, then threw it into the trunk of the car after almost shoving some innocent bystander off the sidewalk. Hopefully it was the B&B owner. As she got into her car he called something out to her, she didn't know what, she didn't care. She'd paid her bill and left her room spotless.

Beth was outta there—as soon as she got out of the passenger seat and into the driver's.

She dialed Lauren before pulling out of the driveway. "I'm coming home!"

"What's wrong? Are you hurt?"

"No! I'm wet, and I'm hungry, and I'm cold, and I'm filthy, and I want to come home!"

Lauren was expecting this call, but that didn't make it any easier. She had been so sure it would be a life-changing trip for Beth. "Head for the airport and I will book you on the first flight home."

"I'm on my way."

"Is it still raining?"

Beth held the phone to her smoking ear and watched the windshield wipers swish back and forth. "Yep. It's still raining," she said flatly. When Lauren didn't reply, Beth said her name to get her attention but still no answer came. In fact, no sound was heard through the line. Beth called out Lauren's name again then looked at her phone. No service.

Terrific.

Beth placed her phone on the passenger seat and sat back staring out the wet windshield. In front of her was a flower garden littered with petals on the ground. Even the flowers had had enough.

Since her phone no longer had service and she did not know where she was, Beth opened the glove compartment of the car and cheered when she found a map. When God closes a door, he opens a window.

She was on the road for only a short while before being redirected because of a flooded road. Even the country had had enough rain. She followed the signs which unfortunately led her onto a rough and narrow road. She had driven other roads just like this and she was perfectly fine, so to speak.

As her car bumbled down the road, splashing enormous waves of muddy water over the roof of the car while tossing her from side to side, everything was perfectly fine.

And it was perfectly fine when the detour took her left, then right, then left, leading her deeper and deeper into the countryside.

Then, she nearly crashed into another car head on.

Frozen, she gulped and clutched the wheel as she stood on the brakes.

She waited, hoping beyond hope the blue car staring at her would graciously back up.

It didn't.

It's fine. Perfectly fine.

She sat up in her seat, nodded her head, and waved her hand signaling she would reverse.

She put the car in reverse, and wished to God she had rear windshield wipers. Had it actually started raining harder?

Beth closed her eyes and prayed hard that she not hit anything then cautiously backed up. There had been a pull-off somewhere, she thought, but with all the rain she couldn't tell.

She watched and finally spotted it. See? It's fine!

She nodded as the other driver waved on his way by.

Perfectly fine.

Beth gave her filthy, soaked hatchback some gas but it didn't move. She tried again and the wheels spun.

Everything is fine.

She closed her eyes and this time instead of praying she yelled. Not the yell of a child having a tantrum but the shrill scream of a woman 7.2 seconds from losing her marbles.

Beth gripped the steering wheel, showing it who was boss then eased on the gas. The car jumped then spun again. She repeated this wonderfully entertaining, physically therapeutic driving sequence over and over until at last she was nearly on the pavement. One more jump and she would be free! Beth hit the gas, hit the pavement, then hit an orange rain jacket.

She jumped from the car and dashed to the orange jacket "Oh my God!"

"There I was going to help you and you're after driving over me!" a man moaned.

"It was an accident! I didn't see you!" Beth knelt beside him in the river of rain and mud and assessed the extent of his injuries and was more than relieved to find that, aside from being drenched, he was fine. "I'm so sorry!"

"That's all right. You didn't hit me too hard." He hunched and groaned again as he stood up and got a look at the American standing in the pouring rain with her arms crossed, shivering. "I saw you were stuck and was coming to help you. I live right there." He pointed to the house only yards away.

A stranger had left the comfort of his home to come out into the rain to help her and she nearly killed him. That 7.2 seconds was up. Release the marbles! "Thank you," she choked, "but I'm," then came the tears, "I'm fine!"

Tears or not she'd said that all with a stiff upper lip, he had to give her that. "Listen, why don't you come inside? You're soaked to the bone."

"No, thank you, I'm—"

"I know, you're fine but," think fast man! "I'm not. I'm having some pain here in my back. Could you maybe look at it before you go?" He laid a hand over his hip and winced.

Beth looked over to the sunny yellow house, whose front was tastefully decorated with pots of flowers in every color and whose chimney puffed warm smoke into the sky. "Of course. Here, get in my car and I'll drive you to your door. Do you need help into the car?"

"No, No." He flicked his hand and carefully got into the passenger seat. Once she was inside, he introduced himself. "I'm Roan by the way, Roan McCabe."

Roan McCabe looked to be about Beth's age, had warm blue eyes, a firm jaw, and a devastatingly handsome smile. Not that she noticed. All Beth could think about was getting to the airport and getting the heck out of Dodge. But, first, she needed to attend to her patient.

CHAPTER
Eighteen

ROAN OPENED his front door and held it for her to pass through. Inside, it was warm, not just the temperature but the feeling of the house. It was comfortable with its sage green walls, carpeted floors, and large stone fireplace. "It's a lucky thing I found you, Bethany Spinner. Another storm is coming in and it's going to be coming down even harder soon. It would have been too dangerous to be on the roads." Roan peeled off his wet jacket then disappeared into another room.

When he returned, he carried a towel and a small blanket he handed to Beth, suggesting she may want to wring out her hair and bundle up. He stood back and while he tried not to watch he couldn't help but notice her beauty. Before he began to stare he walked away and turned on the television to show her the weather map. So much for flying home.

Beth took her phone out of her pocket to call Lauren. Still no service. She was alone in a stranger's house, in the middle of nowhere, on a street that was washing away with each passing minute, in a storm, and nobody knew where she was. This was less than ideal.

"What's wrong?" Roan asked.

"I don't have any service and I need to call Lauren."

"The tower was damaged in the storm so that's why your phone doesn't work. Is Lauren your husband? Is he here?" he asked.

Roan was easy to talk to, or Beth didn't care. Her will to live was hanging by a thread. Either way she flung her entire biography at him. "No. I'm not married and I don't have a boyfriend either. Lauren's back home in Minnesota and was booking me a flight home but seeing as I can't get to the airport …" Just then a loud clap of thunder echoed through the sky. So loud it made her jump. "Does it ever stop raining here? I mean, enough already!"

"You know, in the Bible it rained for forty days and forty nights and they called it a disaster? Here we call that summer." It was a joke and a good one but she hadn't so much as cracked a smile. He cupped the back of his neck. Something told him that Bethany Spinner was about to fall apart.

"What was I thinking? Coming here? Alone? Not knowing anyone! I wanted an adventure! Well, I got one! I haven't slept in days! I'm tired, I'm wet, and I just want to go home!" Hey, if she was going to be murdered by this handsome stranger, she wanted to get it over and done with and whining might do the trick. "I really screwed the pooch."

Roan coughed a moment. "Excuse me? You did what?"

"Screwed the pooch? It means I messed up."

Roan shook his head with a small chuckle. "Well, I may be able to help."

"I don't see how. Unless you know a way to get me back to Minnesota today."

The poor woman was clearly done in. Aside from being a sopping wet mess, her eyes had circles black as the ace of spades. "No, but I have a house that's sitting empty. My grannie died a couple of weeks ago and she left me her cottage. You could stay there for the night. It's just down the road. You would have passed it. The blue one on the right."

Beth's head knew to be skeptical but every other sense was screaming to take the place for the night, lock all the doors, bolt the windows, and sleep with a knife at her side just in case.

As water dripped down her hair, over her shoulders, down her back, and into her lap she nodded and agreed. She looked around the kitchen and on the wall was a picture of him with a woman who could only be his grandmother. Any man who kept a portrait like that couldn't possibly be dangerous. And if he was, she prayed he killed her quickly. "I haven't looked at your back yet."

"I have a confession to make. I lied a little bit about my back. I just wanted to get you out of the rain is all."

If he was a killer, he was smooth.

"You can follow me over there in your car now, if you like?" Roan went to the pegs hanging beside his front door and seeing as an umbrella would fold in this rain, pulled down a dry jacket for her to wear.

Throwing caution to the wind, Beth unwrapped the towel around her hair and set back out into the rain with Roan.

True to his word, there was a bright blue cottage with a bright yellow door, smiling in the rain, just down the road.

"What a charming home," Beth said as she passed through the front door into a room brimming with memories.

"Charming? You really think that? I always thought the place looked like the airport lost and found." Roan shook off his wet coat so as not to track water everywhere then turned up the furnace.

"Are you kidding? It's beautiful." Beth eased out of Roan's jacket and handed it over to his waiting hand. "Are you sure about this?"

"Sure. You look honest enough. You could have driven away after hitting me but you didn't."

"I'm really sorry about that."

"No need. I was in the right place at the wrong time. Anyway, I think you're safe. There's not really anything of value here so I doubt you'll be sacking the place."

Funny, he'd been sizing her up like she had him. Beth turned a full 360 degrees, gazing at the room. The love this woman had had for her family radiated from the colorful walls adorned with family pictures mixed with various works of art, mostly of Irish landscapes. The pictures were vibrant and stirring with their sweeps of green and waves of blue. They were also a big sham. It was amazing how an artist could take such a dismal place and make it look like the Garden of Eden.

"Grannie was an artist. Many of the pictures you see are hers."

A painting of a long-haired white cat made her smile as the memory of rambling to Aidan about becoming a crazy cat lady played in her memory.

"That's her most recent cat, Mr. Jameson, he ran away the day she died. We tried to catch him but he didn't like anyone but her. He's deaf, so couldn't respond to our calling."

"And now he's missing? The poor thing must be scared to death."

"Yeah, that's if he's still alive."

Beth didn't want to think of the innocent, lonely pet wandering around in this perpetual rain. "Deaf? Really?"

"That's right. Can't hear a thing. He enjoys singing and playing the piano though."

He'd said it with such a straight face. Beth wasn't sure if he was kidding but either way it was funny.

Roan stuffed his hands in his pockets and looked around the ever so familiar room. "Grannie never made any money from it. She painted for herself."

"Your family didn't want her paintings?"

Roan chuckled as he crossed the living room into the kitchen, filled the teakettle with water, and turned it on. A hot cup of tea would see her right. "Each of us have all her paintings we want. I have at least a dozen myself. My mum must have over twenty, my sister the same."

With exhaustion creeping up her spine, Beth made her way to the kitchen and sat down on a stool at the island in the center of the floor. From there she had what might be a pretty view of a garden if it weren't for the weather. A large glass sliding door led onto a small patio and from there it was one step before one would be enveloped in flowers.

"I never got around to disconnecting the house phone and that should work fine. You can use that." He wrote the phone number and address of his grandmother's house and his own number and drew her a map to the nearest grocery store. Of course, he wanted to know more about her, for more reasons than one, but she was dead on her feet. Best to let her rest.

Before leaving, Roan brought in her suitcase and surprisingly, didn't remark how heavy the case was, and started a fire, then ducked out the front door into the storm.

Beth locked the door behind him then fell back against it. Beside her, on the wall was another painting of the elusive Mr. Jameson. The thought of him outside alone and scared made her uneasy. "Well, I must reek of loneliness and despair. Maybe you will come to me?" She watched the flames dance inside the fire-place for a moment then went to kitchen door, opened it and stepped onto the covered patio, calling his name. She waited a few minutes but when the largest lightning bolt she had ever seen cracked the sky, she jumped inside, locked the door, and closed the curtains. No cat would be out in this storm anyways.

As the thunder and lightning continued to brawl, fatigue was catching up with her. If she was going to call Lauren, she needed to do it now.

"Beth, what happened? Are you okay? Are you hurt?" Lauren cried into the phone. She hadn't even asked who was calling. "I was looking up how to contact the Irish authorities!"

"I know, I called as soon as I could. The storm damaged the tower so my cell phone doesn't work now. The landline works though."

"Did you make it to the airport?"

"No!" Beth's tears came fast and furious. She hadn't made it to the airport, no instead she got lost, stuck in the mud and hit a guy with her car! She was stuck on this God-forsaken island probably forever!

"Slow down and tell me what happened. Where are you? Are you safe?"

"I don't know!" she bawled. "In some adorable cottage in … somewhere!" Bethany repeated her story as slowly as she could, enunciations and all—but all Lauren heard was a noise like a cross between Charlie Brown's teacher and a donkey in heat.

Seeing that Beth needed a minute to compose herself, Lauren stood up from the bar stool in her kitchen, put the phone down and brewed a pot of coffee, then came back and sat down and raised the phone to her ear just in time to make out the words, "It really was nice of him."

Lauren placed down her hot coffee gently. Sure, if "gently"

was the definition of spilling it all over your lap and sinking your teeth into your fist to stifle your screams of scalding pain! "Him? Who's him?"

Beth said nothing, she was too busy blowing her nose.

Lauren tipped the receiver tight to her lips. "Bethany Anne Spinner! Pull yourself together and tell me! Who. Is. Him?"

Bethany pulled the phone away from her ear while she was yelled at then stopped blowing her nose. "All right, jeez Louise! Keep your socks on!"

That message came through loud and clear. Lauren blinked and dropped her fist from her mouth.

"*He* is Roan. The guy who very, very kindly offered me his grandmother's cottage."

"Why is that very, very kind of him?"

"Because he offered it to me five minutes after I ran him over with my car."

"You what?" Good thing that scalding hot coffee was already cooling in her lap because if it wasn't it would be now.

"Yes," Beth said in a small voice.

"But, he's okay?"

"Yes."

Beth's tone didn't exactly earn a vote of confidence. Lauren couldn't think with all these wet, screaming hot, clothes singeing her skin. She told Beth she would call back in two minutes, then raced to get a change of clothes.

Beth hung up the phone and blew her nose, then turned to the kitchen sink and splashed water on her face. As she patted her face dry with a tea towel a knock sounded on kitchen door. Beth jumped at the sound and looked up to see Roan standing on the patio holding a basket.

She dried her face as best she could and swallowed her tears then slid open the door.

"You've been crying?" He didn't step inside. On the patio he was sheltered from the rain.

"Yes, but I'll be—"

"You'll be fine. So you say but twice I've seen you and twice you're crying."

Beth looked away, her bottom lip trembling, and smoothed her hair.

"Listen, I won't stay but I brought you this." He handed over the basket. "Call me if you need anything, anything at all." He nodded a goodnight then disappeared behind the wet curtain pouring from the roof.

Beth pulled aside a blue plaid tea towel to reveal groceries. Eggs, milk, butter, orange juice, apricot-infused cheese, grapes, a homemade loaf of brown bread, a container of warm stew, and a bottle of wine. Underneath everything was a note.

Bethany,

In the cupboards are tea, coffee, jam, and such. Help yourself. Here are a few things to get you through the night. I didn't much like the idea of you driving to the shop in this storm. I made the stew and bread myself. I'm no Darina Allen, but I do all right. Call me if you need anything.

-Roan

Roan, once again, had left the comfort of his home to offer help.

When Lauren called back she was surprised Beth was speaking English again. That was a relief. Lauren didn't know anyone who spoke donkey. "Help me out here. Two minutes ago, you could hardly speak through all the snot coming out of your nose. What's changed?"

"Roan stopped by as I hung up the phone. He brought me groceries and dinner and a bottle of wine."

"This is the same guy that you hit with your car?"

"Yeah. Isn't that sweet?"

Sweet? Was she serious? The man had already seen Bethany at her worst and he still offered her a house and dinner? Either he was Prince Charming in the flesh or he was an ax murderer fattening up his prey.

Lauren got Beth to repeat the entire story from the beginning. Unbelievable.

Even for Beth.

"You hit him with your car?"

"Yup," she said with an unamused popping P.

Beth's trip couldn't possibly get any worse. Lauren didn't know whether to roll on the floor laughing or burst into tears.

"There's no internet here so could you book me another flight home?" It didn't matter what seat or class, she just needed to get out of this country.

Beth's trip had been one big Maalox moment. Anyone would have given up ages ago but not Beth. She always was the brightest star. Nothing could put out her light. But now, Lauren heard it. Beth had given up. And who could blame her? But something told Lauren that Beth wasn't meant to return just yet.

I mean, who wouldn't want their best friend to marry a charitable, handsome Irishman who forgives when he's hit by a car? He couldn't be more ideal.

"Of course, I will. I'll get on the computer right now." Lauren walked into her office and sat down at the computer, then placed Beth on speaker phone and took hold of the mouse.

Within a few clicks she found a flight home for the following day—or so she said. Lauren didn't actually know what flights there were. She was redecorating the master bedroom and was currently viewing sheets. "Crap."

"What's wrong?"

"The flight is full."

Of course, it was. Poor, exhausted, at-her-wits-end Beth sighed. If she wasn't already bone-weary she would have cried again but right now all she had the strength for was surrender. "I can wait another day."

How many days could Lauren get away with stalling before it sounded suspicious? "The next flight isn't for another two days."

"Okay, book me that one."

Lauren weighed the options, calculated the consequences and risks … to click or not to click?

Either way, it would be an adventure. She wanted to see where this Roan guy was going with his basket.

Lauren clicked the mouse. "Done." Yeah … all she had clicked on was the purchase button for the Egyptian cotton purple sheet set she'd been eyeing.

"Thanks."

"I'm sorry this trip has been so hard. But you'll be home soon."

Beth squeezed her shoulders together. "Home." It wasn't just a word, it was a feeling. One she missed desperately.

Beth headed for the bathroom. She would have felt guilty for not admiring the house more while passing through but her head was gradually falling off her shoulders. She needed sleep and a shower—not in that order.

Once she was dried, she borrowed a pale blue cotton night-gown from the closet, climbed inside the bed, and was asleep before her head hit the pillow.

CHAPTER
Nineteen

A POLKA BAND had played an all-night concert inside Beth's head. Forgetting where she was, Beth squinted her eyes open and reached around in the dark until her hand touched a lamp on the bedside table and turned it on. With her eyes squinting in the light, she looked around the charming bedroom with its blue flowered wallpaper and white cotton ruffled curtains.

On the far wall were paintings. One of the larger ones was of a long-haired white cat with bright blue eyes laying on what appeared to be the very bed she was in. Now she remembered: Roan.

She should at least drink some water. Her eyelids wanted desperately to be closed again but her eyes were like sandpaper.

Beth crawled out of her warm, soft bed and made her way to the kitchen where she opened only two cabinets before finding the glasses and filled one with water from the tap. As she stood, leaning against the island drinking her water, she noticed how quiet it was. No thunder, no lightning, only a light rain, the fire wasn't even crackling anymore.

Then she noticed the empty basket and remembered: Roan had made her dinner. Beth's eyes were barely slits but her stomach growled at the smell of food. Go back to bed or eat? She tore off a hunk of the brown bread and ate it, not expecting much, but it was delicious. Her stomach won the debate.

Within a few minutes Beth had a hot dinner all plated and was happy to find there was still a fire left to salvage and all it needed was a couple of fresh logs and a little poking.

Beth brought her meal to the living room and placed it on the coffee table, then sat on the sofa, crossing her feet underneath her. Behind her was a quilt draped over the back of the sofa that she dragged across her lap, then ate her delicious dinner in front of a crackling fire.

As Beth ate, she gazed at the pictures on the mantel. There was one of Roan holding up a large fish, and another of him on a mountain bike. There was a family portrait taken in front of a large Christmas tree. It was typical: some people had sunny smiles but with their eyes closed, others looked perfect, and where were they … She scanned each face looking for … ah ha! There was always one person rolling their eyes, usually a child. In this one it was a little redhaired girl with freckles and hair as bouncy as Shirley Temple's. Beth grinned at the child with a twisted face and wearing a ruffled red dress. Her tongue was sticking out, her arms crossed, and apparently, Santa had not brought what she wanted.

There in the center of everyone, seated in a chair, was an older woman with white hair loosely pulled back and up. She had a kind face, a welcoming smile, and a twinkle in her eye. Beth surmised she must be Roan's grandmother. She looked at the other pictures and off to the left was a small black and white wedding portrait.

Beth placed her empty dish back on the coffee table and got up to get a better look at the photo. Although the bride was decades younger, there standing on church steps, holding a bouquet of roses was the white-haired woman from the family portrait. Even in black and white the twinkle in her eye could be seen. The groom was very handsome and proud in his army uniform and his best girl on his arm. It must have been a windy day because her veil was blowing off to the side. Beth looked back over to the Christmas family portrait. The happy couple had made a beautiful family.

How nice for them.

With a heavy sigh Beth took her dirty dish to the kitchen sink, filled her glass with water, gulped it down, filled it again then headed back to bed. She was tired and although the stew had weighed down her crankiness a notch, it was still off the charts.

———

Beth awoke to knocking on the front door. She stretched her arms out from underneath the quilt and one by one slung her legs over the edge to the floor. She didn't need a mirror to know that her hair was sideways, backwards, and every way in between and that half of her face showed wrinkles from the pillow. Not that she cared. Who was she trying to impress? Wrapped in the quilt, she bumbled her way to the knocking at the door.

Beth swung open the door and was blinded by the daylight. Through the purple spots in her eyes she tried to make out who was on the doorstep. "Roan? What time is it?"

"About half past two. I stopped 'round this morning but you must have been sound asleep."

She covered her mouth and yawned. "I haven't slept this

well in weeks." Her brain began to fizz and wake up. If it was daylight outside, then that meant she had slept through the night and more than half of today. "Did you say half past two? I'm sorry. I should be gone by now. I'm so sorry." She turned and began walking away still apologizing before he could get a word in edgeways.

"Bethany, wait. You don't have to leave, love."

She stopped rambling and turned back around.

"If you like it here you can stay."

"You would let me stay another night?"

"Another night, another week, a month. Whatever suits you."

"You would rent me your home?"

"Sure, I would. The house was just sitting empty anyway. Besides you would be doing me a favor looking after the place. You can think about it and let me know."

Beth didn't know what to say. He'd made the offer so freely. His generosity came so unexpectedly that she forgot about her flight.

"Listen, on the off chance that you might stay," he gestured to the bench outside beside the door where a bag sat. "I brought you dinner."

She was still speechless.

"I'll be off now and let you rest. We can work the details out later." He gave a reassuring smile and turned to leave. "The tower isn't fixed yet but the sun is coming out."

"Roan," she blurted. Finally getting her power of speech back. "Thank you, for all this."

"You're welcome, love. You can call me if you need anything. Anything at all." He pursed his lips then put his hands in his pockets and headed to his car, whistling. The dark clouds were finally lifting, and the sun was reaching down, stretching its arms.

Beth stood, wrapped in the quilt, her mouth gaping. Roan really was a nice guy. But she was much too tired to expand that thought now. She brought the bag inside and took a whiff. Whatever Roan had cooked smelled divine. With a grateful heart, she put the dish in the refrigerator then headed to the bedroom where the soft, warm bed beckoned.

CHAPTER
Twenty

BETH'S EYES OPENED. It couldn't be said that she opened her eyes, because if she'd had any say in the matter her eyes would remain closed for a week and even that may not be long enough. But there her eyelids were, open. And now that her eyes were open, she saw that, once again, she had slept through more than half the day. Only this time she didn't feel like she'd been hit by a freight train. In fact, once her senses all got on board with being awake, she decided she felt pretty good, and she was starving.

Her breakfast comprised of orange juice, brown bread, yogurt with a banana, and strawberries, and when that didn't fill her up, she ate some chicken kiev with mashed potatoes.

There. Now that her stomach was satisfied, and she felt more human it was time to get herself looking more human.

She touched her hand to her hair and cringed. She didn't need to look in the mirror to know it was a poofy, frizzy mess. Time for a shower.

Once she dried off and brushed out her hair she went to her

suitcase for some clothes. As she lifted the lid the smell of horse assaulted her nose—some clothes were dirtier than others. Time to locate the washing machine. And since she was the only one in the house, Beth didn't see any reason she should put the nightgown back on.

So, Beth padded through the house naked. She hadn't walked around naked in … never mind how long.

The washing machine and dryer turned out to be under a counter in a small laundry room off the kitchen and were much smaller than what she was used to, which meant it would be hours before she had clean, dry clothes.

Beth started up the machine, then headed for the clothes closet. The nightgown she had borrowed fit well enough. Maybe there was something else she could put on for the time being. Nice as being nude was, she was getting a little chill.

She passed by the sliding glass door in her kitchen and looked out onto the garden. Now that it wasn't raining, she could go outside and get a good look.

A privacy fence surrounded the garden blooming with yellow, purple, and pink flowers. She knew nothing about plants so she couldn't identify any of the flowers but she could appreciate their beauty.

Beth opened the door and was about to step outside when the crisp air caught her unawares. She grabbed her shawl that laid over the kitchen stool and draped it around her shoulders then stepped out into the open air.

"Good morning," said Roan from the gate.

Beth shrieked and pulled her shawl tight around her.

"I'm sorry. I should have knocked on the front door. Old habits die hard." He leaned against the fence. "Do you always walk around outside in your nick?"

Did he always act so casual around naked women? "Nope.

First time." She couldn't look him in the eye and anyway those yellow flowers with the pink face were ever so pretty and really needed to be admired.

"Sorry I scared you. I was only dropping by to leave you these. I picked them while I was out for a walk." He pulled a bouquet of wild flowers from behind his back. "There's a blue vase sitting on the counter. Grannie always liked to have flowers in it. She said they made her happy and that it was the simple things that can turn a day around. So, I thought you might like these." Without taking a step closer he leaned forward with his arm outstretched.

She gripped her shawl and reached out a hand to accept the bouquet. "They're beautiful, thank you." She dared a glance at his face and couldn't ignore his amused eyes.

"I'll leave you now to commune with the fairies." He turned to leave but stopped at the garden gate and looked over his shoulder. "You look really good naked, Bethany Spinner."

She blushed all the way to her toes.

He turned again to leave, then paused. "Also, I wanted to ask, that is, I wondered if you might like to go to a wedding with me on Saturday. You could meet some of your neighbors there. It should be great craic."

She knew from her book that craic meant fun. "Lauren got me a flight home tomorrow."

Roan's disappointment reflected in his eyes. "Oh. That's good. You'll be happy to get home, I'm sure." He shifted his stance. No sense in lingering now. "You can leave the keys in the kitchen when you go. If you want help with anything you can call me." He looked into her eyes, held her gaze for a moment. "I'm sorry you weren't happier here."

"Roan. Wait." For a moment she forgot she was naked underneath a shawl. "Wait here for a minute, would you?"

He turned back around then perched his arm against the garden gate and nodded as she went indoors to find some clothes.

When she returned, she wore the blue cotton nightgown. If she was trying to look less appealing her attempt failed. All her lack of finesse had done was make her appear relaxed and carefree and that look agreed with her.

Her fingers appeared from under the overly large cuff and tucked her wet curls behind her ear before speaking. "Would you like to come in for some tea?"

"Sure," he said with a friendly smile.

Beth led the way indoors then filled the tea kettle with water and placed it over the burner on the stove.

Roan was filling the vase with water, not watching what she was doing. "You know, most girls would have been so embarrassed they would have run inside and avoided me at all costs."

"I've had enough embarrassing moments in my life that I'm over it." She opened a cabinet and pulled down the canister of tea and two cups and placed them on the island. "If I ran away every time something embarrassing happened to me, I would stay locked inside forever."

Roan chuckled as he placed the vase in the center of the island and sat down.

Beth admired the flowers a moment and the vase they were placed in. She hadn't noticed it before but it was hand blown teal glass. "Did your grandmother make this vase?"

"No, glassblowing was one thing she never did. I think one of her friends made it. Grannie knew all sorts of artists."

"She must have been a fun lady."

"She was," he said thoughtfully. "Grannie died only a month ago at the ripe age of 97." It was then an odor reached his nose that had him spinning around. The kettle was melting on the stove. In two long, strides he turned the fire off and dropped the kettle in the sink under running water.

It had all happened so quickly, Beth hardly realized what was going on.

Roan turned around from the sink with a dumbfounded look.

"I, I don't know what happened! I'm so sorry!" Beth wrung her trembling hands.

"It's all right. No real harm done. I'll open this door to get the smell out." Roan opened the sliding door, letting the fresh air do its work. "I suppose you don't have electric kettles in America?"

Beth's eyes darted around the room. "Yes, yes, we do. I made tea every day for years. My kettle goes on the stove. Roan I'm so sorry!" Her tears were fast and furious.

"Hey, it's all right. No worries. Let's chalk it up to force of habit. Accidents happen."

"But I could have burned your house down!"

He placed his arm around her shoulders and walked her to the nearby rocking chair. "You wouldn't have burned the house down. I'm sure of that. Everything is fine."

"It's not fine!" she wailed.

What he needed was a distraction. "Beth, love. Stall the ball."

"What?"

"It's an Irish phrase. It means slow down." His distraction worked. In her confusion she stopped crying.

Then, of course, the phone rang. Seeing that Beth was in no condition to answer it herself, Roan did. "Hello?"

"Who the hell are you? Where is Beth? What have you done with her?" an irate Lauren yelled.

"Beth is right here. She's crying. I didn't hurt her! I swear!

We had a minor accident in the kitchen is all and she's shaken up."

"Put her on the phone now!"

Roan eased Beth's hand away from her face and placed the phone in it.

"Beth? Honey what happened?"

"Lauren! I started a fire!"

"Are you okay?"

"Yes."

"Is the house okay too?"

"Uh huh."

Lauren exhaled. Okay, just another clumsy moment. "Who was that that answered your phone?"

"Roan."

"Who is Roan?"

"This is his house." Oh, *that* Roan! For heaven's sake this was taking much too long to get answers out of Beth. "Put him back on the phone, would you?"

Beth handed the phone to Roan. He braced himself for another yelling. "This is Roan."

"Have you got a last name, Roan?" Lauren demanded.

"McCabe."

"And you live up the road?"

"Yes."

"And this is your grandmother's house Beth is staying in, not the home you keep your tourist victims shackled in? Is there a basement? A secret room? Hidden cameras? A shed in the woods?"

Jesus, this Lauren woman would put the fear of God in the Pope himself! "I swear to God my intentions are honorable and nothing nefarious is going on. Bethany invited me in for a cup of tea then she got turned around and accidentally put the electric kettle on the stove."

Yep, that sounded like Beth all right. Okay, he was telling the truth. No more need for the tenth degree. "Thank you for helping her."

"It caused a little smoke. No real harm done. Listen, I'm going to leave and let you two talk."

"Thank you, Roan."

Before leaving, Roan picked up a box of tissues from a desk in the living room, handed them to Beth and quietly let himself out.

"Roan said everything is fine and no harm was done," said Lauren.

"I know but ..."

"Go and eat some of that fruit and cheese." Lauren figured she wouldn't mention the stove. Everything else would need heat.

Still on the phone, Beth ate and drank as Lauren suggested and now things didn't look as grim.

"Lauren, I was having a nice morning. It's not raining for a change, and I slept so well. I was finally comfortable here." Beth took another drink of orange juice before relaying what happened next. "So comfortable that I was walking in the garden—naked."

It didn't take Lauren but a second to put two and two together. "Roan saw you outside? How much did he see? Does he know the carpet matches the drapes?"

"Yeah," she drawled.

"That's more action than you've seen in—"

"I know how long it's been, thank you for reminding me. Could we focus please?"

"Here's what you're going to do. Wash your face with cold

water and get dressed, then you're going to the store to get your own groceries and you're going to make some chicken soup." Beth made the best chicken soup. This would take care of two problems with one solution. Beth would have to use the kitchen stove again, and she would make herself some nourishing food.

"I still have some stew from Roan and I'm flying home tomorrow. I don't need groceries."

Lauren crossed her fingers and prayed silently for forgiveness before delivering her lie. "Actually, your flight got cancelled." She winced, waiting for Beth to respond. This could get ugly.

Beth poured herself a drink of water and took a sip while looking outside at the colorful garden and replayed the scene of being naked in the sunshine. Her skin warmed at the thought. "That's okay."

Beth's voice wasn't all that disappointed so Lauren didn't feel terrible when she told the second ever so small, teensy white lie that the next flight wasn't until Sunday.

Beth trusted her friend explicitly so if Lauren said there wasn't another flight home until Sunday then there wasn't.

"I guess that means I could go to the wedding."

"What wedding?"

"Roan invited me to a wedding on Saturday."

Lauren hugged the phone receiver tight to her chest while she squealed. This is exactly what Beth needed. "I think you should go. You can tell him after you've gone to the grocery store."

Lauren wasn't always so bossy but Beth was in no state to make her own decisions at the moment. At least not the decisions Lauren wanted her to make.

CHAPTER

Twenty-One

ONCE INSIDE THE GROCERY STORE, which was thankfully small and therefore manageable, Beth got a cart and began reading the aisle markers. First, she needed a chicken. She spotted the butcher counter in the back and headed in that direction. Everything was going fine until she turned a corner and crashed into another cart. Without looking at the person pushing the art, she apologized and backed away.

"Spinner?"

Beth looked up and into familiar eyes. "Aidan!"

The delighted surprise in her eyes warmed his heart for a moment. If he was honest there hadn't been a day he hadn't thought of her but dammit he didn't want to think of her! And now here she was, crashing into him! Again! He hardened his stare and must have hardened it too much because she suddenly shrunk away from him. It wasn't his intention to intimidate her. He scolded himself, and softened his tone. "What are you doing here?"

Her head dropped and what little smile was in her eyes

disappeared. Although his tone wasn't so harsh his eyes were blazing annoyed so she answered him while looking at the selection of bread on the nearby shelf. "Buying groceries."

Duh. "I meant what are you doing *here*. You never said you were coming to Kenmare." He'd just scolded her, again, even though he hadn't meant to. The first words Beth ever said to him rang in his ears. He didn't need to be so mean about it.

"I didn't mean to!" she cried. She looked him square in the eye that time, then moved her cart out of the way of another oncoming shopper. "I got lost in the storm the other day and then there was the accident!"

"You were in an accident?" Aidan's irritation disappeared completely.

"Sort of." Ashamed, she gripped her cart's handlebar a bit tighter for stability when what she wanted was to throw herself into his arms and sob. But she couldn't do that, not again. She lowered her eyes and, with all her might, willed her tears to dry up.

Something was wrong. Aidan could feel it. Beth wouldn't look at him and her knuckles were so white it wouldn't surprise him when the handlebar bent. He wanted to ask what was wrong. Could he take her for a drink? Did she need a hug?

Of course, she needed a hug, dammit!

Nope! Not going there, remember? "At least you're having that adventure you were looking for."

"Not really." All the thoughts she'd had about slapping him disappeared. Beth raised her head and met his eyes. The bluest, most sincere eyes. She would miss them, but at least she got to see them one last time. "I'm going home. Ireland isn't for me. I'll stick to the Ireland I know in your book."

Beth was leaving?

If Aidan wasn't fighting his feelings for her so hard, he

would have actually heard his heart crack. He sure as hell felt it though.

NO.

He had to get away from her before he said or did something stupid. "I'm sorry it wasn't everything you wanted it to be. I hope you have a safe flight. Take care, Spinner. It's been fun—meeting you." He nodded his head in goodbye and left, marching straight out the front door, leaving his full cart behind and Beth wondering what she'd said to make him run off in such a rush. Humph, he was probably trying to avoid being run over by her—again.

Beth blinked a couple times, then shook her head. Authors sure were moody people. At least this one was. He was right though, it had been fun meeting him. A picture of Aidan laughing came to the front of her mind. He had a great laugh.

Well, that's enough of that.

She didn't think she would ever see Aidan again but there he was and she got to say goodbye, more or less. She couldn't ask for more than that.

With a nod, Beth straightened her back and squared her shoulders. It was time to navigate the grocery store. Her stomach growled in agreement.

In fact, it agreed so heartily that by the time Beth left she had enough food to feed an army. For. A. Month. Looks like she'd be eating her feelings tonight! Anyone have a problem with that?

She returned to the charming blue house and remained in her driver's seat, with her hands and her jaw in her lap, gawking at the colorful display of the perky flowers basking in the radiant golden sun.

Pfft, whatever. Where was your beauty last week Ireland, huh, huh? It's too little! Too late! I'm leaving!

With her nose in the air and her arms full of groceries, she marched past some pansies and through the doorway after bursting it open with her ass.

As she forced the groceries into the refrigerator she was snapped out of her momentary weakness to beauty. Why in God's name was this fridge so tiny?

Beth stepped back from the refrigerator that came to about thigh-height and stomped her foot. Fine. Her stomach reminded her she didn't need to put everything away because it was hungry and had feelings to eat.

She sat down in the chair and ran her fingers over the green painted table.

She frowned, then looked around, taking a mental picture of the inviting kitchen. The vibrant paintings, the various colored glass figurines and vases placed strategically on the window sills so color would shine onto the wall when the sun came out, like today. There were two empty plant stands. Of course, Roan would have removed the plants if nobody was living there. Beth wondered what beautiful houseplant they'd once been home to. Then there was the small, well used butcher block island that currently carried the weight of her groceries. And across the table at the empty space was the bottle of wine from Roan.

Beth looked at the island heaped with food and her stomach rumbled again. If she didn't eat something soon it was going to get mad but really, instead of having a pity party, what she should do is something to make up for nearly burning down the house.

Beth picked up the phone and called Roan with an invitation to dinner that evening, which he accepted.

CHAPTER
Twenty~Two

WEARING an apron she had found in the pantry that said "Never trust a skinny cook," Beth ladled soup into a large bowl for herself while Roan sliced the bread she had baked. "I didn't make anything all that special. I would call it comfort food."

"It looks great and smells even better," Roan said as he tore a piece of warm bread from the loaf. The bread, whatever kind it was, was perfect and when he tasted her humble soup his eyes rolled back in his head. Maybe Beth couldn't drive but she sure could cook!

Roan and Beth had a friendly dinner. She mostly asked questions about him and talked little about herself no matter how hard he tried. But it wasn't long before he could tell she was getting tired. He would have happily stayed long into the night and maybe opened that bottle of wine but he knew when to leave. Besides, he would have her all to himself soon enough.

Once dinner was done and Roan helped with the dishes he said, "What you need is some couch-melting relaxation."

"I-uh-what?" Did that sound like what Beth thought it

sounded like? Was Roan coming onto her? Should she be grabbing the nearest blunt object?

"You know, your favorite movies, some wine and snacks, a soft blanket."

"You mean be a couch potato? Thank God."

"Yeah. Why what did you think I meant?"

"Nothing!" She certainly wasn't mapping out an escape plan. "Is there somewhere I can get a few movies?"

"Inside the closet of the yellow room are rows and rows of DVD's."

Beth went to the yellow room and felt around for a light switch but couldn't find one.

"Roan, where is the light switch in this room?" She stepped inside the room but couldn't see much except a bed. In a moment Roan was behind her.

"There isn't a switch here, there's a lamp here on the table." He bent down and turned on a table lamp.

"I offered to put in a switch for her but she wouldn't have it. The stubborn old cow."

Beth snickered at Roan's display of loving sarcasm. "Are you an electrician?" She realized then how little she really knew about this guy—aside from that he was handsome, benevolent, and a good cook.

"No, a general handyman. I have my own business and sometimes I work for another company on large jobs."

Beth nodded and followed him to the closet. "Ta da! I present you with a personal stash of DVD's.

"Jeez Louise, that's a lot."

"Grannie loved films. Her favorites are on that shelf." He gestured to the eye-level shelf. *Gone with the Wind,* all of the *Rocky* films except five, *The Gods Must Be Crazy,* every movie

John Wayne ever made, *It's a Wonderful Life* ... and *Fifty Shades of Gray!*"

Beth looked at Aidan and giggled. "I wish I'd known your grandmother."

"She was a character. She would have liked you."

"I think I would have liked her too.

"So, what's your pleasure?"

Beth looked over the titles and selected Gone with the Wind. "It looks like your grandmother had a good sense of humor."

"Aye, she was a character all right. One time she snuck outside my bedroom window making animal sounds like something big. When I went to the window to check, I found someone wearing a clown getup. Anyway, I didn't know it, but it was her and she grabbed me. I nearly shat myself and there she was laughing so hard she could barely breathe. She nearly fell off the ladder. And she did that only a week before she died!" He was kidding, of course, but said it with a such a straight face he would have passed a polygraph.

That did it. Beth howled at the idea of an old woman dragging a ladder and climbing up to his window. She rocked back on her feet and laughed, then tripped over her own two feet, stumbled into a table, and knocked a lamp onto the floor. Much to her relief, it didn't break.

"She was from Sneem. Have you been there?"

"No why?"

"You'll feel like you stepped through the looking glass there. I guarantee you won't understand a word they say."

"Come on."

"No, no I'm serious! Ask anyone around here. Pretty village though. They have a very nice hotel as well if you fancy being pampered. You'll see it for yourself on Saturday at the wedding."

"That place sounds nice but Lauren got me a flight home for Sunday."

"You're leaving? Is this about the driving? Because I can teach you to drive."

"No, it's not just the driving." Although, she couldn't deny that was a big part of it. "I don't fit in here. It's funny, my favorite book is set in Ireland and I always dreamed of coming here, to see the places in the book, breathe the air, hear the music, enjoy the culture … but I want to go home."

"Have you seen anything?"

"Not really. A friary, and I saw the tomb. How do you say it? The Poulnabrone Dolmen Portal Tomb."

"I've never even seen that."

"You haven't? It's so cool! It's the oldest tomb in the world! Even older than the pyramids of Egypt!"

Beth's tone had changed from bummed out to exhilarated. That wasn't the tone of someone ready to leave. "I never knew that."

"It's true! It was huge too. Those stones weigh tons. I can't even imagine how they built it. Twenty-two people were buried there and there were artifacts too like pottery, and jewelry and weapons. I think that's what the signs said. I almost broke my leg falling between those big flat rocks. That is really interesting landscape there with all that limestone. The Burren they call it, right?"

"That's right. So, what else have you been doing?"

"Staying in my room ordering room service, watching reruns of *Columbo* and *Murder, She Wrote*."

"You can always find one of those playing here. Angela Lansbury lived here, you know?"

"She did?"

He nodded his head. "In Cork somewhere. The story is,

when she took residence the local crime rate dropped because the locals didn't want her to investigate."

Beth couldn't help it. That was funny. She laughed, then laughed some more.

"Where else have you been here?"

"I walked around Ennis a few times and saw the friary there, and went into a few shops." She decided that mentioning that she had nearly driven through some of those shop windows wasn't necessary.

Roan waited to hear more of her excursions but after the shops she stopped talking. "Is that all?"

Beth nodded as she took a bite of the bread she had just buttered. Ireland may not agree with her but Irish butter sure did.

So, all she had seen was the inside of a few hotel rooms, rain, and a bunch of reruns on television. "I could take you on a drive. We could go tomorrow."

"You must have a life and I've interrupted it enough but thank you. No, I'm just going to chalk this trip up to a terrible decision. But it's ended so much better than it began. Roan, I can't thank you enough for letting me stay here. It's the first time I've felt comfortable since I got off the plane."

"I'm happy to help. So then I'll come by for you on Saturday at three."

"Oh wait, Roan what kind of wedding is it? I mean is it black tie?"

"No, just wear something nice and you'll be grand. See you."

"See you," she smiled to herself. Bethany Spinner had a date.

CHAPTER
Twenty-Three

BETH STARED at her reflection in the bathroom mirror with a terrified, helpless expression. Her long loose curls that normally laid nicely, must have been attacked by a flock of birds during in the night. Another reason to go home. Her hair had never looked like this before. She dialed Lauren.

"Help! My hair is awful! What am I going to do?"

Beth had the nicest head of hair Lauren had ever seen so she didn't take her seriously. "How bad can it be?"

"Remember the time you crimped my hair?"

"Yes ..." Lauren was afraid.

"This is worse."

Be afraid. Be very afraid.

Beth really was having a bad hair day! And that's a whole lot of hair to have a bad hair day with! There was only one thing to do, Beth would have to be brave, and ever so cautiously use bobby pins. God preserve us.

Luckily Beth found some bobby pins in a small box on top of

the dresser. One thing every woman has is bobby pins—unless your name is Bethany Spinner.

After thirty minutes of instruction, two dozen pins, and some hairspray that made Beth sneeze, her hair was elegantly pulled back and up. Crisis averted. Only now she had just a few minutes to apply her makeup and get dressed before Roan arrived.

Lauren wished her luck and blew a kiss through the telephone.

A knock sounded on the front door and Beth rushed through the house in no shoes, while putting her earrings in, to answer it.

"Wow, you look gorgeous," Roan said after she threw open the door. Bethany Spinner cleaned up nice, really nice. Her pulled-back hair exposed her elegant neckline, and her teal dress was sexy without being revealing. In short: Wow!

"Thank you." She didn't realize his compliment was genuine or she would have blushed. "I'll just put my shoes on and get my purse. I'll only be a minute." She hurried away, leaving him in the living room to roll up his jaw.

While he waited Roan thought how nice it was to have life in the house again. His grandmother's house had always been a warm, inviting place but lately had been cold and empty and it felt wrong. Now, with Beth there, the house—its spirit—was alive again.

"Okay, I'm ready." Beth reappeared holding her jacket (she wasn't taking any chances), purse and wearing black satin flat shoes with a rhinestone buckle.

Roan smiled in appreciation and offered his arm to escort her to the car. "It's another nice day outside. Hopefully you won't need your jacket," he said, opening her car door.

Beth thanked him as she slid into her seat. His car was clean, comfortable, and a standard shift. She shuddered at the sight.

Roan got in and backed out of the driveway. As he waited for a car to pass by he took a moment to admire Beth. "Your hair looks nice like that," he said.

"Thanks. I had to call Lauren for help on what to do with it." Suddenly Beth realized she forgot her phone. The cellular service had come back on and she wanted to have it with her—in case she was dead wrong about Roan and he did in fact turn out to be an ax murderer.

Roan pulled back up to the house and Beth jumped out, hurrying into the house. She was only inside for a few seconds before reappearing, slamming her skirt in the door, and hopping back into the car.

"There was no need for you to rush like that," said Roan.

"I didn't want to make you late." Beth shut the car door, buckled her seatbelt and pulled her purse onto her lap, then realized it was stuck. "Ope! I shut my purse strap in the car door." She opened her door, gathered her strap, and sat back. Only this time she caught her jacket that was draped over her lap in the door.

She opened the car door once again to retrieve the jacket, then somehow ended up dangling out the door with her face a few inches from the gravel.

Roan leaped from the car and went around to her.

"Are you okay?"

Beth blew a few stray curls out of her face. So much for all those bobby pins. "I think so. What happened?"

Roan helped her sit up then noticed her jacket had snagged on the seat lever. He pulled it free then asked to see her hands.

"Roan, I'm a nurse."

"And I'm a concerned man who would like proof your palms aren't bleeding."

Beth held out her palms. Aside from a few temporary pits from the pebbles, they were intact.

"Now turn your wrists for me and wiggle your fingers."

"Roan I—"

"Please?" She did as he asked. "May I?" He reached for her hand and she nodded. With the utmost tenderness, he felt around her hands for any injuries.

Watching Roan made her think of hitting him with her car and swiping Aidan off his feet. At least Roan had walked away unscathed and Aidan had appeared to be back to being Mr. Grumpy Puss.

Satisfied that Beth wasn't injured, Roan grinned and backed out onto the street.

"Good thing it was only my purse this time and not my dress."

"Why, has that happened to you?"

"Yeah …" she sighed. "Twice my skirt has gotten caught in the car door and twice the car drove away along with my dress."

"So, you were left standing naked in the street then?"

Beth nodded her head. "That's right. One time I was on a date, he never called again, and the other time was at my best friend's wedding."

"That would be Lauren?"

"Yes."

"She sounds like a good friend to have looking out for you. She put the fear of God in me and all she did was ask my name."

"Yeah, that's Lauren."

The car went silent for a minute and all that was heard was the grating sound of the road.

"So, was it your bridesmaid's dress that got caught in the door?"

"That's right." Beth looked out the window at the stony, uphill countryside passing by. In the field was a flock of sheep, all with a bright blue circle on their wool. They looked content as they grazed on green grass and bright colored wildflowers. She thought back on the memory from Lauren's wedding and smiled. "It was June first and couldn't have been a more beautiful day. There was a long white limousine, really fancy inside. I'd never seen the inside of a limo before." Suddenly she heard Aidan's voice in her head interrupting her saying, "And the cat ran away with the spoon." He'd meant that as a joke, right? Or did she really talk too much? Okay, maybe she had talked a little too much. But she was scared, okay? Give her a break! Just in case, she didn't want to bore Roan with the details so she got to the point. "Anyway, luckily the driver didn't get too far before Lauren caught up to him and my dress was fine." The memory of Lauren hiking up her poofy wedding gown with her enormous bouquet in one hand then running after the limo waving her massive bouquet like an air traffic controlman and shouting was one of the funniest memories of their thirty-three year friendship.

Now Roan understood why Beth hadn't freaked out when he saw her naked. Bethany Spinner was a bit of a handful. But a handful he was happy to have beside him in his car. Although, getting her to talk much was still a bit of a challenge. Maybe a fun evening would help relax her? After all, she hadn't liked one bit of her trip to Ireland and yet, there was no mistaking the change in her these past few days. She wasn't afraid or worried with exhaustion. She was well rested and relaxed, more or less.

Yes, Roan was confident that a fun night out would be just the ticket.

With that said, they spent the rest of the twenty-five minute drive mostly in silence, and listening to the radio.

Rain was coming, stocks were up, and U2 were on the first leg of a new concert tour. Jesus, were those guys still touring?

Roan and Beth arrived at the swanky hotel in Sneem, and man Roan was not kidding when he said it was "very nice." Very nice didn't do it justice. It was modern luxury nestled beside a brilliant tranquil cove. Beth sighed and smiled. What a perfect place for a wedding.

Before Roan parked the car, they were met by a parking attendant. Roan rolled down his window and the man spoke and pointed. Roan rolled up the window looking confused. "Did you understand any of that?"

"Not a word."

"Neither did I. We'll find the wedding ourselves."

The hotel was like a palace but before joining the wedding, Beth needed to wipe off her purse before she got dirt on anything. Roan pointed her toward the ladies' room and she excused herself.

Roan waited near the front doorway looking around the room at all the familiar faces nodding and smiling in friendly greeting. It was good to get together every now and again. His gaze stopped at the face of an old friend approaching and he smiled wide.

"Roan, how have you been? I was beginning to think you weren't coming."

Roan gestured a hello with his chin and shook hands. "Hi, Aidan, did I miss the ceremony? Oh, what a shame." He was familiar with how this marriage would most likely go and to be honest didn't want to dedicate an entire day to another one of Heather's eejit dossers. "Anyway, I'm not bad, and yourself?"

"I'm here, aren't I?"

"Remind me, what's this one? Husband number four, right?"

Aidan nodded his head and pinched the space between his eyes. "He's twenty-seven, a folk musician, and plays the uilleann pipes."

"So, he's broke as a joke."

"She really screwed the pooch this time."

"That's funny. I'd gone my whole life never hearing that but that's the second time this week I've heard that expression. The girl renting Grannie's house said it."

"Here she is now." Roan held his arm out to introduce Beth but she recognized the man first.

Aidan raised his drink to his lips and froze. The ice cubes burned against his skin.

"Aidan?" she said. Cripes!

"You two know each other?" Roan asked.

Aidan swallowed an ice cube—Jesus Christ did that burn—and nodded, lowering his glass. "In a manner of speaking."

"Fate has conspired against me," Beth muttered louder than she'd intended.

Aidan leaned in closer to Beth. "That's funny. I was just thinking the same thing, Spinner." He leaned back and crossed his arms.

Awkward.

Beth and Aidan both had the same hard line across their face. Desperate as Roan was to know how Beth and Aidan knew each other—hey just because he was a man didn't mean he didn't enjoy a good bit of gossip now and then—Roan sensed that they had something to work out. Maybe they could use a minute? "I'll just get us some drinks while you two catch up."

Aidan took Beth by the arm and led her away from the crowd that was moving in. "What are you doing here?" He hadn't meant to sound so demanding. But there it was.

Aidan sounded irritated but his eyes said something different. Beth wasn't sure what that something different was, but she
sure would not stand there in the middle of a wedding and
argue about it! Or would she? "You know, that's exactly what
you said the last time you saw me? Roan never told me whose
wedding this was!" she hissed.

"I meant in Ireland! You're supposed to be back in
Minnesota!"

"My flight was cancelled, okay?"

Fine. She didn't control that. But that still didn't explain why
she was on the arm of the local heartthrob handyman. "Well,
how did you meet Roan?" That condescending tone of his was
back in full force.

"Why did you say it like that?"

"Like what?"

Beth raised one eyebrow and put her hand on her hip in
reply. All she left out was tapping her rhinestone buckled foot.

No matter how sorry Aidan was, and he was sorry all the
way down to his toes, he couldn't stop the hurtful, and if he
would get real, jealous, words flying at top speed from his lips.
"Fine! The other day you said you were miserable and leaving
so obviously you move pretty fast! So you must be having a
good time now!"

Beth's eyes grew wide and dark as she leaned in, scolding
him. "I do not! Roan invited me and I said yes! I've never been
out with him before or anybody else here!" Why was she
defending herself? No matter, she wasn't finished. How dare he!
"And you wouldn't know a good time if it fell on your head!"
Whoa! Where did that come from?

Her sudden outburst turned him on. Beth had all but
stomped her foot when she said it and Aidan had to fight the
smirk that wanted so badly to curl. He cleared his throat and

softened his tone. Beth really was painfully adorable when she got angry. "I seem to bring out the worst in you."

"I'm sorry. I don't know why I said that." Any other time she would have been mortified at her outburst but all she could think was how satisfying it was to drop the gauntlet.

"It's all right, I had that coming. I'm sorry too. Can we be friends?"

She avoided making eye contact and instead, stared at the twinkling fairy lights draped in the splendid vase of white with the palest of pink and peach roses displayed on the sideboard in front of them.

"Come on. Please?" He stuck out his bottom lip. Sure, it was childish but he was desperate and would pull any straw necessary to get her forgiveness. "Just think, you would be friends with your favorite author."

"Your ranking is quickly declining." She clamped her hand over her mouth. "I'm sorry! I don't know why I said that either!"

"Like I said, I bring out the worst in you." He smirked and she grinned. "I'm sorry your flight got cancelled."

She nearly said, "Why, because you want me gone so badly?" but the puppy-dog face he was now giving her was too pitiful for words. She couldn't stay mad at that face. "Of course, we can be friends." Not that it mattered, really. After this, she wouldn't ever see him again. So why not part on good terms? Beth exhaled and leaned back, shoulder to shoulder, against the wall beside Aidan, her purse dangling between her knees.

"The bride is my sister," he said in an easier tone.

"If you must know, Roan is my landlord."

Oh, right. Aidan forgot. Now, if it were possible, he was even more sorry.

He shared a look with Beth. Of all the towns in all of Ireland

...

Seeing Aidan calm down, Beth relaxed. "I'm here because Roan needed a date, and he's nice, and I kind of owe him."

"Why do you owe him?"

Beth looked sideways to all of the guests, smiling, dancing, dressed in their party clothes and pursed her lips. "It was an accident," she muttered. With her it always was. "I sort of hit him with my car."

Oh, *that* kind of accident! A Bethany Anne Spinner Ride or Die accident. Just as Aidan's jaw dropped open, Roan appeared, cautiously, carrying three glasses of whiskey. After the daggers the two had had in their eyes he didn't know whether to expect bloodshed or to find them making out in the corner. He was relieved it wasn't either.

"So, are we all friends now or do I need to fetch another round?"

"No need." Aidan accepted the glass Roan offered him and held it.

"But you may need to erect a ring." Beth half-smiled at Aidan and he smiled back, laughing in his throat with a nod. Arguing had never been so satisfying.

Roan looked from Aidan to Beth wondering what on earth was going on. When they didn't offer an explanation, he held his glass out in front of him and gestured for them to clink their glasses together in a toast "To new friends and new beginnings."

"Cheers."

"Sláinte."

While Aidan and Roan only took a sip, Beth downed her double shot in one gulp with a small gasp from the burn. That was really smooth whiskey! Within seconds she was blissfully lighter. "I'd better not drink anymore. That's going to my head already."

"Oh no. You're not going to sing again, are you?" Aidan teased.

Beth blinked her eyes a few times fast. "When did I sing? Did I sing?"

Aidan was about to take another sip but lowered his glass from his lips. How could she forget singing? "How much do you remember of the plane ride?"

And just like that, Roan was caught up. They had met on the plane!

"Everything, I think. Why?"

"Does Patsy Cline ring any bells?" Aidan asked, nodding.

She stared at the floor and thought but nothing sprang to mind. "I didn't sing."

"I'm telling the story and I'm telling you, you used an empty bottle of Jameson as a microphone."

Jeez Louise! That was something she only did when she was alone! Beth cringed. "Sorry. I tend to do that when I'm really nervous or drunk."

"One guess, you were both."

She thought hard but didn't remember singing. She must have been more drunk than she realized. No wonder he'd asked how much she remembered. She cringed again. "I'm sorry. That really was a harsh flight for you, wasn't it? But you were so kind."

"I wasn't kind, I was an asshole."

Yeah, Roan thought that sounded more like Aidan. Aidan used to be the nicest guy anyone could know but ever since he was dumped that nice guy showed up less and less.

Beth laid her free hand on Aidan's arm and gently squeezed. "I don't remember that. I remember a stranger listening when I needed an ear and who offered his sympathy, made me laugh, and who tucked me in so I wouldn't get cold."

"He did all that?" Roan asked but wasn't heard. Or he'd been ignored. He wasn't sure which.

Beth and Aidan only looked at each other and she still hadn't taken her hand off his arm and Aidan didn't exactly look like he was hating the tender gesture. Being overlooked, Roan decided it best to remain a quiet observer.

"I did all that?" asked Aidan.

"I probably wouldn't have gotten off the plane if it hadn't been for you."

"Sure, you would've. You were brave enough to get on. Why wouldn't you see it through after coming that far?"

He'd paid her a compliment. That was suspicious. There had to be an insult in there somewhere but he'd said it so easily. "You think I'm brave?"

"Yes, I do." Aidan held Beth's stare for a long moment. Those twinkling eyes of hers were so ... Nope! Not going there! Eyes left, Turner! Look what an attractive spray of flowers. Were those lights in those roses?

Suddenly, Aidan couldn't decide what to do with his free hand: Stuff it in his pocket? Hold his lapel? Run it through his hair? Beth quickly took back her hand, then spun the ice in her glass, staring at it as if it were a hypnotist's pocket watch.

What exactly happened between these two on the plane? It was hard to tell if they liked or despised each other and Roan knew all too well, there's a fine line between love and hate.

Beth was about to say something when her phone vibrated inside her purse. Knowing it would be Lauren, she excused herself and went outside to take the call.

Roan watched Beth walk away while Aidan struggled not to. After all, those really were little lights weaved through those roses and how clever was that?

Perhaps now that Beth was gone, Roan could get some

answers. He gestured to the empty table nearby and they both sat. Roan looked around the room. Heather always knew how to throw a grand party. "So, you're the author Bethany was telling me about?"

"Her favorite author?"

"No, the one who wrote a book filled with, how did she put it? "Oh, yeah, 'A flim-flam patty, sandwiched between lies and more lies, topped with deceit, and served with a side of fraud.'"

"Ouch. Yeah, that's me." That seemed harsh and out of character for Beth. Her trip must have been worse than she'd made out. Not that he'd given her a chance to explain before running out on her. "She really said that?"

"Yeah." Roan watched Aidan's jaw clench. So, her opinion of him mattered. The question was: how much? "But I suspect it's because she'd had a little too much to drink and all."

Aidan shook his head with a chuckle. "Yeah, she's a chatty one when she's had too much to drink."

Roan lowered his glass from his mouth. "She is?"

"What?"

"You said Bethany is chatty."

Aidan recalled their plane ride and snorted. "She could talk a dog off a meat wagon."

"She can? I haven't known her to be chatty except maybe after she hit me and was upset." And really that had been more of a nervous breakdown than a Chatty Cathy demonstration.

Aidan didn't know what to say. Roan must enjoy having his ear chewed off, the poor devil. Although, he hadn't minded it much either now that you mention it.

"She's funny," Roan said.

"Yes, she is."

"And smart."

"Yes, she is."

"And beautiful."

Aidan half nodded with a thoughtful grin. Was Roan going to list every one of Beth's attributes? If so, why not do it alphabetically?

"And clumsy as a two-legged dog."

"Yes, she is."

They shared a chuckle.

Yes, she really and truly was. It suited her though, somehow. If she weren't clumsy, she would be too perfect. Aidan thought back to the story of her walker incident and falling into an open grave. He chuckled, picturing her being pulled out from a six-foot hole by her friend. "Did she tell you about Lauren and her grandmother?"

Roan nodded slowly. "I met Lauren, over the phone."

"Really? She sounds like a character."

"She's terrifying."

Aidan snorted. Of course, Lauren was terrifying. Beth was too damn nice to be friends with more nice people because even those nice people wouldn't be half as ... as ... nice as Beth! Of course, Lauren was scary! Beth needed to brighten someone's life, didn't she? She couldn't let miserable, frightening people just be miserable and frightening, could she? Nooo! She just had to stumble right in, and knock you on your ass with her lovable, blushing face, her sunny smile and that damn twinkle in her eyes, and melt your frozen heart!

Take a breath.

Perhaps, it was time to lay off the bar for a while? Aidan cleared his throat and placed his glass on the table. "Did she tell you she dropped her suitcase on my foot then spilled her drink on me then swiped my legs out from under me with that same beast of a suitcase?"

Roan blinked—twice. Jesus, that was a lot for a single day,

but two could play this game. "You just went arse over teacup. At least she didn't hit you with her car."

Aidan and Roan both howled with laughter. There was a clear winner of this match.

"What's so funny?" Beth asked, surprising them both.

Roan pulled himself together first. "We're just sharing some memories is all, love," he said and glanced at Aidan whose shoulders were still shaking with laughter. Then his phone rang. What a rude interruption. He sighed and apologized as he looked at the incoming call. "Sorry, I need to take this. I shouldn't be a minute. I'll just step outside."

Beth nodded and clutched her hands in front of her as Roan walked away. She looked so lonely standing there holding her brown purse. "Was that Lauren on the phone?"

Beth nodded. "Yes, she checks up on me a lot." Aidan gestured to the empty chair and she sat down, looking around the room at the couples dancing, and sighed. It must be nice … "So, how do you know Roan?"

"He dated my sister for a summer a while back."

"And she invited him to her wedding?"

"They were never serious and parted as friends. He's been invited to all her weddings."

Beth couldn't understand that arrangement but it wasn't any of her business either.

There Aidan was, alone again, with Beth. He didn't know if it was the booze or the jubilant atmosphere but that didn't bother him now. Aidan slapped his hands on his lap. "How about it? Why don't you take a whirl around the dance floor with me, Spinner? You know, in the spirit of our truce?"

All Aidan's mixed signals were making Beth's eyes cross, but she put her purse on the table and stood up. Confused or not dancing would be better than sitting around drinking. Before she could actually say any of that to him, he had her hand, pulling her along to the dance floor.

"You know, Turner, you're very bossy."

"Spinner and Turner. That's funny. I hadn't thought of that before. If I were writing a story, I might think the similarity is too cutesy."

"We aren't a couple so how can it be cutesy?"

Beth was cutesy. Everything about her was cutesy. Except that sexy dress she was wearing. "You clean up pretty good, Spinner."

Aidan was impossibly handsome and charming when he wanted to be and right now, he wanted to be. She didn't even notice that he already had her inside his arms, swaying.

As the music played her shoulders dropped and she settled into his arms. Without noticing she rested her head against his shoulder and closed her eyes. As Aidan swayed her on the dance floor everything melted away and all that was left was music, warm shimmering lights, the scent of roses, and his comfortable embrace.

"See that older man at the bar in the hat?" he asked.

Her eyes blinked open as if coming out of a trance. She looked towards the bar and spotted him. "Yes."

"Watch out for him. He likes to pinch women."

"Pinch them?"

"Right on the arse, as they say here." A woman passed by the man and shrieked. "See, I told you."

Beth giggled. It was music to his ears.

"Your head is okay, right? You didn't have a concussion?"

"My peripheral vision came back yesterday," he teased.

"And how's Ernie?"

Aidan chuckled. "Ernie, well, he's enjoying himself right now."

Beth giggled some more and they fell into relaxed silence.

Then Aidan spotted a guest on the floor that reminded him of the helmet-haired stewardess and speaking only loud enough for Beth to hear, pointed her out to Beth. "What is that she's doing?"

"I think she would call it dancing. But it's supposed to be waltzing, not pole dancing."

Aidan laughed. "That's my girl." She rested her cheek against him again, enjoying the music. "You're surprisingly light on your feet, Spinner."

"I am?" Beth looked down and sure enough, she was standing on her own two feet and not his. That had never happened. Her memory flashed back to the senior prom when she caused a multiple person pile-up with her two left feet. Her classmates had gone down like dominoes.

Beth was brought back to reality when again she heard a woman's shriek ring out. That dirty old man! And speaking of men doing things they shouldn't: "Will your girlfriend be upset that you're dancing with me?" she asked.

"What girlfriend?"

"The woman who met you at the airport."

"That wasn't my girlfriend. That was my sister, Heather."

"Do I hear my name being taken in vain? Who's this, Aidan?"

Aidan stopped dancing but didn't let go of Beth's hand. Whether or not that was intentional was a different matter for standing beside them was the bride waving a half empty champagne flute, plastered in makeup and nearly plastered with booze. It was also the same woman Beth had seen throwing herself into Aidan's arms at the airport. Beth wasn't sure if she was relieved or not but she definitely felt foolish for jumping to conclusions. Especially since Heather's breasts didn't look nearly as big as they did at the airport. She was a beautiful, elegant bride—on the outside.

"Bethany Spinner, let me introduce the face of Kate Connolly and also my sister, Heather. Heather … what's your last name now?"

Heather stuck her tongue out and was about to fire back at her brother when what he'd said sunk in. "Bethany? The woman from the plane? Cupcake?" Heather couldn't believe the lucky coincidence. A mile-wide smile brightened her face.

"Beth is Roan's date."

The smile on Heather's face hardened. "Excuse me?"

Beth looked up at Aidan with a jeering grin. "You told your sister about me?"

"No, I complained to my sister about you." That's his story and he's sticking to it! Just ignore the goofy smile splitting his usually crochety face.

"It's nice to meet you, Heather. This is such a beautiful wedding and your dress is gorgeous."

Heather struck a pose for the pretty redhead. Maybe she had passed over her brother but the woman knew good taste when she saw it. But that didn't change the fact that Beth had come on the arm of somebody else but was now holding her brother's hand. What did this two-timing, red haired hussy think she was doing?

"Heather, love, stop standing like you're in the Miss America pageant. And give me this." Heather tucked her glass tight to her body. A tall, elegant woman wearing a lavender chiffon dress wanted it, but she would not get it.

Aidan huffed when their little trio was interrupted by none other than his mother with his father right behind her. Did anyone else want to join in? They could have a square dance. Good grief. You try to have just one dance …

"Bethany Spinner, these are my parents, Greg and Pamela."

"Bethany?" Pamela looked at her son with a gleam in her eyes and shared a knowing look from over her shoulder with her husband. Pamela had observed the smile on her son's face from across the room. He hadn't smiled like that in ages, and had come to drag Heather away before his smile disappeared again.

"You know mom, the smiling, happy, bulldozer from the plane that dropped her suitcase on his foot, spilled her drink all over him, almost broke his nose and then cried, got drunk and talked for almost twelve hours then knocked him out—and I believe she ran over Roan with her car. The whole town is talking about it," Heather said. Nobody passed over her brother and got away with it!

Aidan's grip on Beth's hand tightened and Beth's lips parted as her cheeks burned with embarrassment.

"Heather!" Aidan scolded.

Humiliated, Beth turned her face toward Aidan and whispered so as not to make a scene. "I shouldn't be here. I need to go."

Before Beth could make a move, Pamela crossed over to her and placed a warm hand on her arm. "Bethany, or may I call you Beth? Aidan told us so much about you, I feel like we're old friends. Please, excuse my daughter. She's had too much to drink and we all know she's a horror when she drinks. Isn't that right, Heather, dear?" Pamela snarled over her shoulder. "Please, stay. We're so glad to have you!"

Greg, who was a man of very few words, held a hard stare at his daughter, shaking his head as he removed the glass from her hand. This was not one of his daughter's shining moments.

Heather rolled her eyes and when they came around full circle and stopped, they narrowed on the concern on Aidan's face. Whether he realized it or not he'd put his arm around Beth's shoulders, as if protecting her from any further verbal assault. Suddenly it all made sense. Yes, Beth truly was owed an apology.

"Beth—"

Without taking his eyes off Beth, Aidan snapped, "Leave her alone, Heather."

Heather clasped her hands in front of her at her waist. "Just give me a chance. Beth, I owe you an apology. Aidan never said that about you. He only said good things, I promise. I was just being over protective."

"And bitchy," Aidan added.

"Yes, and a total bitch. I really am sorry." When neither Aidan or Beth so much as looked at her, she nodded her head. She wouldn't forgive anyone who had been so insulting either. "Listen, I hope you'll stay. It's going to be a splendid party, and I'd really like it if you'd let me make it up to you. I'm really nice."

"When you're not being bitchy," Aidan added.

"Yeah." She waited, almost expected to be forgiven but when neither said anything she turned to leave but turned back when Beth spoke.

"Heather, wait. Thank you."

"So, you'll stay?"

Beth looked up to Aidan and nodded with a smile.

Aidan put his other arm around Heather's shoulders and squeezed her in close to his side.

"You were right, Aidan. She has a kind heart. And I'm sorry," she said, kissing his cheek.

Aidan smiled. "Stop sucking up. I'm not buying you another coffee maker."

"Come on! Please?"

"You already lost two in your divorces."

"It is a really nice coffee maker, you can't blame them for wanting it." Heather looked around Aidan's chest to Beth. "Beth, don't you think a big brother should give his baby sister a gift for her wedding?"

"Absolutely they should!" Beth said.

He was outnumbered. Aidan looked at Beth, then his sister, and relented. He'd already bought her the stupid coffee maker anyway.

Victory! "Beth, if you're still in Ireland when I get back from my honeymoon, I'd like to take you to lunch! And make sure you line up when I throw my bouquet! I want you to catch it!" With a glint in her eyes, Heather pecked her brother on the cheek again. "And Beth, watch out he doesn't try anything. You're just his type." She may have said it in a mischievous tone but she meant every word. On that note she left, swishing her way through the crowd, kissing everyone's cheek.

"So, that's your sister?"

"Yep, that's Heather."

"She seems nice. You know, when she's not defending your honor."

"Sometimes I wonder if she's just here on this earth to torment me." Having never left the dance floor, he pulled her hand, turning her into him. "Now, I believe, before we were rudely interrupted, we were sealing our truce with a friendly dance."

She nearly said no but those bright blue Irish eyes—the ones she couldn't stop staring at since the first time they met—were pleading. And they had called a truce after all. "Fine, all right."

He grinned in triumph and wrapped his arm around her waist. "So, are you enjoying the wedding so far?"

"It's a good thing I'm going home tomorrow. I seem to cause you trouble every time we meet."

Aidan stumbled on her feet. "I'm sorry, I have two left feet."

"I know the feeling."

Aidan wanted to say something. Anything. But nothing came out.

"Sorry about that, Beth. I didn't mean to be so long." Roan appeared beside them. "It was my sister on the phone."

Aidan and Beth stopped dancing and he released her. "I hope everything is all right?" Beth asked.

"Yes, thanks. It's nearly time to sit for dinner. How about we find our table?"

Beth smiled and nodded, saying goodbye to Aidan and thanking him for the dance.

Aidan half turned to walk away. Beth was leaving tomorrow. She was Roan's date. They had made a truce and could now part on at least friendly terms.

That was enough.

He wasn't looking for anything more so why prolong the inevitable?

But holding her had been so damn nice.

He turned back but she was already being guided to a table by Roan's hand on the small of her back. Roan was good guy. He would watch out for her and be good and generous.

Yes, it was enough.

CHAPTER
Twenty-Four

LIKE HELL, it was enough! The thousand-yard stare had nothing on Aidan. Throughout the delicious six-course meal Aidan had tried and failed to not look at Beth. Thanks in part to the fact that she was directly in his line of sight. He would have switched seats if it wouldn't have placed him beside the maid of honor who never kept her hands to herself.

Aidan sat and ate and drank and observed Beth smiling, laughing, nodding—then laughed himself when she pulled the wrong napkin off the table and flung silverware all over the table. She was relaxed, enjoying herself. And he was stuck kicking away a roaming high-heeled silver shoe. Exactly how long were that maid of honor's legs anyway?

Finally, the last course was served and eaten which meant he was free to go—after he finished the last bite of whatever this chocolate dessert was. As he spooned his rich chocolate dessert into his mouth he thought back to the plane when they had ordered double desserts and combined the fruit with the chocolate. He wondered if she had done the same with Roan. He looked over to her table, watching and waiting to find out.

No, she hadn't.

He shoved back from the table and kissed his mother good-bye, intending to say he would see her and his father at home, then quickly slip away. Pamela had other ideas.

From her seat, she caught his face when he kissed her and held him close, digging a fingernail into his skin just enough to command his full attention. "You wouldn't be trying to sneak out early, would you, love?"

Ouch! Aidan puffed his cheeks and blew out a breath. "Come on, Mom. I'll tell you what. Let me slip away and I'll cook your favorite meal tomorrow." The way to his mom's sharp, French-manicured fingernail was through her stomach.

Pamela smiled and dislodged her fingernail but remained cupping his cheek. She loved her son's homemade meatballs and sauce. If he hadn't been an author, he could have been a chef, but being a mother meant making sacrifices and right now she was about to sacrifice a perfectly wonderful meal. "Why don't you ask Beth to dance?"

He stood up and backed away. "Could we not discuss this?" All he wanted was to get the hell out of there. Why was that too much to ask?

She could have shouted at him but there was no need to make this a public conversation. Pamela stood up and stepped to him. "I didn't say you should marry her." Although she wanted to. "Just dance. You weren't enjoying yourself at all until Beth arrived and she obviously enjoys being with you."

"Obviously?"

"Come on. She doesn't look at Roan the way she looks at you."

"And how does she look at me?"

"Her eyes practically dance! Don't try and tell me you haven't noticed." Pamela knew he wouldn't be pushing Beth away if he hadn't noticed.

Aidan looked over toward Beth to see for himself and was disappointed to find her seat empty.

"All I'm saying is, enjoy yourself for once."

Uh-huh. If that was all she was saying then he was the Sultan of Kathmandu. "Would you stop pushing?"

"Well, love, somebody has to. You can't sulk forever."

"I'm not sulking!"

"Sure, you are. And it's become worse since you got here. If you ask me—"

"I'm not asking you."

"But—"

Aidan mushed his fingertips into his forehead. He loved his mother. She had the kindest heart of anyone, but so help him ... "Mom, I'm begging you. Please, leave this alone."

"All right." She kissed his cheek where she wanted to slap him, turned, and sat back down.

Something was up. She'd given up too easily. Pamela Turner never obediently sat down and did as she was asked. Never.

Who cares! Get away while you still can!

He'd nearly made it to the front door when the call of nature rang. Fine. A quick piss, then go!

Once through, he zipped up his trousers, washed his hands, and—almost home free—dashed out the door, crashing into Beth, who was leaving the ladies' room.

"Now who's doing the crashing?" she teased.

"Sorry about that. Are you okay?"

"I'm fine."

There was a moment of awkward silence before either spoke. He needed to leave but he didn't want her last memory of him to be him running out on her yet again. "Did you enjoy dinner?" Aidan asked.

"That was the most delicious meal! Did you have the chocolate dessert or the raspberry?"

"The chocolate. I thought about getting both."

Of course, he had. She'd remembered ordering two desserts on the plane too. She didn't mention that she had offered to split hers with Roan who had the chocolate torte but he'd declined. The spoiled sport. "I ate more than I should have."

"Nonsense. Life is too short not to enjoy yourself—or so they say." Her perfect heart shaped smile lit up her face. He would miss her smile. There was another awkward moment of silence before Aidan spoke again. "Listen, enjoy the rest of the wedding and I hope you have a safe flight home." With a nod and a quick smile, he turned to head for the nearest exit. At this point he would jump down a manhole if that's what it took to get him out.

"Are you leaving?"

"Yeah, weddings aren't really my thing and Heather won't mind."

Beth cocked the corner of her mouth. She didn't know Heather well, but something told her she would mind very, very much.

Aidan flicked his hand in the air. "Okay, Heather won't mind until she realizes I'm gone and that won't be for a long time." After which she will string him up by his toenails and rip out his nose hairs one by one. Which would be marginally less painful than watching Beth enjoy herself with Roan.

Heather was going to find out about Aidan's absence a whole lot quicker than he'd anticipated.

Should Beth tell him Heather is in the ladies' room? Probably. I mean, that's what smiling, happy people do, right? They warn others away from trouble.

Beth couldn't say what possessed her but right then she kept his sister's whereabouts to herself. Clearly, he was intent on leaving, why stop him? "Well, thank you for the dance and everything else. I wouldn't have made it without you." Her sweet face smiled at him as she stood on her tip toes to softly kiss him goodbye on his whiskered cheek.

He hadn't seen that kiss coming. The place on his cheek where her soft lips had touched his scruffy face turned warm and he got warm and gushy inside. Like all he wanted was to throw his arms around her and sweep her off her feet.

Oh, come on! All he wanted was to leave, go home, and drink cider until he couldn't pronounce it!

Bullshit. All he really wanted was to dance with Beth again.

Then Heather appeared in the ladies' room doorway. "Aidan, there you are. I was looking for you."

Aidan looked at the angel-faced traitor, Beth, with his tongue in his cheek. He may have had that coming.

Elbows bent, she raised her hands and fluttered her long eyelashes, feigning innocence.

"You were looking for me in the ladies' room?" he said, still looking at Beth.

"No," Heather sneered. "I made a pit stop." She pinched his sleeve and tugged. "You have to dance with Kim."

"Nope. Not on your life."

"Come on Aidan, please? She's dying to dance with you and you're such a great dancer. You know how much I love seeing you dance."

"Yes, dear sister, I know. I also know that I just rubbed Kim's foot print off my thigh."

That was not an acceptable excuse. "I'll tell her to keep her hands to herself. But the maid of honor always dances with the best man, you know that." She was whining.

"Heather, I just met Joey last week. I don't think he knows I'm his best man. I'm not even sure he knows who I am at all. Therefore, I do not. I repeat do not feel guilty for saying no."

Heather appealed to Beth. "Beth, help me out here, would you?"

"She's right. It's tradition."

Aidan pursed his lips together. Beth was full of it today!

"It's only one dance. Just a few measly minutes to make your sister's wedding perfect. How bad could it be?" With that, Beth excused herself.

Heather waited until Beth was out of earshot before leaning close to Aidan and speaking low. "Beth's much prettier than you described. And so, so nice! I knew she would be."

"How's that?"

"Because you try too hard not to like her. She's exactly your type but better. Sweet expression, red hair, sincere eyes, on the thicker side, and she's got a great ass—"

"All right, all right. Can we change the subject? Don't you have a new husband to annoy?"

Heather wanted to tell him the conversation she'd had with Beth while at the ladies' room sinks. If she wasn't mistaken Beth had a crush on Aidan that she was fighting just as hard as he was.

She should tell him. Right? That's what sisters do. They tell their brother that the woman he's secretly in love with probably loves him back.

But she knew her brother. He needed to figure this out for himself. She mushed his face between her hands and kissed him on the mouth with a loud smack.

"Hey, hey, hey! Baby, you're not supposed to be kissing other men at our wedding!" The half-in-the-bag groom shoved his way between the siblings.

"She's my sister," Aidan said over the guy's shoulder.

The groom looked at Aidan, then back at Heather. The resemblance couldn't be mistaken. Apologizing, he excused himself to the gents.

Heather shook her head. "He is pretty, isn't he?" She feigned a swoon. "Good thing. Lord knows he isn't the sharpest tool. It probably won't last but it's going to be a hell of a ride!" She took a few hurried steps away then turned back, waving her finger in the air. "Dance floor. Now. Like Beth said, how bad could it be?"

Eight minutes later Aidan found out just how bad it could be when he removed Kim's stroking hand from his hairline. Then his chest. Then his ass. Would it kill the band to play faster so he could get out of there?

Pamela stood on the outskirt of the dance floor watching her poor son be fondled in public and after a sufficient time had passed —he needed to suffer first— she approached Beth, who was sitting at a table. She greeted Roan warmly then appealed to Beth. "I have no right to ask this of you but would you mind cutting in and saving my son from that octopus? Heather wants him on the dance floor and I know he would stay if he were dancing with you."

"I suppose I could …"

"Wonderful! Just tell her I need to see her and I'll take care of the rest."

Beth couldn't understand why Pamela was asking her but she didn't want to be rude, so with Roan's blessing she crossed the room and tapped the octopus on the tentacle—that P.S. had rhinestones on the fingernails—that wasn't groping Aidan.

The octopus reluctantly released Aidan and slithered away.

"You're a lifesaver!" he said.

"Your mother sent me over. She thought you could use rescuing."

He looked over Beth's head to his meddling mother who was definitely up to no good and scowled. She simply smiled and twiddled her fingers at him then walked away.

Thanks mom.

Well, after all, this was what he'd wanted. And it got him away from that horrid maid of honor. "Roan doesn't mind you dancing with me?"

"He didn't say so. I told you, we aren't a couple."

"So, you're staying at his grandmother's house? I always liked that house and she was a real card."

"You knew her?"

"Not very well but yes. My family's home is right up the street from you about a half-mile. Did she still have that white cat? She was always sitting outside with that cat in her lap."

"Yes, but Roan said he's been missing since she died. I had kind of hoped I would find him but that's silly. I'm leaving tomorrow."

"I'm sorry your trip wasn't what you had hoped for."

"It's okay. I came, I saw, now I'm leaving and I can put away all my stupid daydreams of Ireland."

"What's happened to make you leave?"

"You don't want to hear my complaints."

"Sure, I do. We made a truce remember? Come on, what happened?"

"Other than hitting Roan … I pulled into a McDonald's drive through backwards."

"As in the out?"

"Yep, mm-hmm. It was pouring rain and dark and I couldn't see very well. The next thing I knew, I was facing a pair of headlights two feet in front of me and a soaked employee was knocking on my window."

"Did they help you out?"

"Yes, it took a few minutes to get me backed out of there, I was probably halfway up the lane, but eventually I got out."

"Come on Spinner, you're a nurse. You're made of sterner stuff than this. You're going to let a couple of mishaps chase you away from your big dream vacation?"

Beth thought for a moment, lining up her grievances in no particular order and once that flood gate opened there was no closing it. She listed everything:

"... You could've mentioned in your book that it's actually very difficult to drive in the left ... and the showers in these bed and breakfasts: I've seen larger shoe boxes ... And they don't have hot water all the time and no heat ... You didn't say how much they swear here ... You might have mentioned that it rains up! As if all the raining down isn't bad enough!"

"My book is not a traveler's guide to Ireland! Who told you to stay at those bed and breakfasts?"

"Nobody but they looked nice. How was I supposed to know they would turn off the heat and hot water? And what's with the fake eggs and the smoked salmon? Yuck! And the—"

"Is there anything about Ireland you've liked?"

Beth pursed her lips. No, no there wasn't. All she knew was she had been let down, and hard.

"Anything else?"

"The tiny refrigerators! You could have warned me."

"When was I supposed to do that?"

"In your book!" Duh.

"Uh-huh. You've clearly given this some thought." He spun her out and back into him.

"I have, yes."

"So, where should this appliance warning fit in to my book?"

"After the robbery but before the pie."

"Which pie?"

"The key lime. That's my favorite scene, you know? The ladies in my book club said they would have thought apple pie would be more appropriate for that scene but I liked you chose key lime."

"Thank you." Talk about dazed and confused! He wanted to clamp her mouth shut but he wanted to do it with his own two lips.

"Why did you choose key lime anyway?"

"I don't know. I guess because it's my favorite."

"It is? It's mine too."

"Have you had trouble with the Irish accent?"

"Not always but sometimes I don't understand a word that's said to me. Like the guy who met us in the driveway here."

"Is my name Rick Steves?"

"I don't know, is it? Have you got another name, Aidan? Or is it, Kate?"

Ah ha! Now she tells the truth. "I knew it! You are upset that a man wrote that book."

"I am not." She looked away as he gracefully turned her out and back into him. "Okay, maybe a little. I don't know why. I'm sorry. It's just, I love your book so much and I always thought that because I liked it so much that Kate and I had some sort of connection. Like if we ever met in real life, we could be friends."

"But you met me instead." And no matter how much he wanted to be, he couldn't be her friend.

"I'm sorry. It's dumb, I know."

"Stop apologizing. It's not dumb. I'm sorry too. You had an idea of who Kate would be, an idea that I planted in your head. Let's chalk it up to good writing that you believed me." They fell into relaxed silence again while Aidan considered what he wanted to say. "Beth?" He waited for her to meet his eyes before continuing. "Why don't you stay awhile longer here in Ireland? What's so great back in Minnesota that can't wait a few more days? It's beautiful here and you should experience that."

Did she hear him right? "I, well ..."

"I could take you out. Show you some sights."

"But you said you were only staying here for the wedding."

"I've decided to stay a little longer. If I can, you can."

The song ended and another began but he didn't let her go and she didn't pull away so he continued dancing to the slow melody of an old, forlorn love song, One I Love.

When I'm awake, I find no rest
Until his head lies on my breast
When I'm asleep I'm dreaming of
My one, my dear, my own true love

"It's an awful thing to say. You were so nice to me. The toast to Gram, and you made me not feel scared anymore. You were funny, and familiar."

"But then I snapped at you."

Beth nodded and frowned as she turned her face away. Maybe she'd deserved to be snapped at. She had clung to him, and although it hadn't occurred to her then, she now realized that he was her friend. Only a friend would let her cry on their shoulder, listen to endless stories, and make her comfortable. Only a friend would apologize.

Aidan was a graceful dancer and not once had she stepped on his toes and now, he was asking her to stay. Of course, she couldn't. What was the point? But him offering meant a lot. "You know, when you're not being a ..."

"A grumpy puss?"

"Yes, when you're not being a grumpy puss, you're very nice. Charming even."

"And when you aren't scared out of your mind and drunk, you're very—"

"Hello, love," Roan interrupted. "I ran into a friend and we got to talking. Come and meet him and his wife." Although he'd said he was fine with Beth dancing with Aidan, he felt she had fulfilled her promise to Pamela. Besides, Aidan had danced with her for how long and he hadn't had her in his arms even once.

Aidan dropped his arms and released Beth to Roan but before she left, she thanked him.

As her hand slowly slipped out of his, his heart groaned. There it was. The sound of him being reeled in. Hook. Line. And sinker.

He watched Roan place his hand on the small of her back, leading her away. She was his date after all. If she didn't want his hand on her then it wouldn't be there. That much he knew about Bethany Spinner. She may need some extra care, but she was no baby.

Aidan huffed a breath through his nose as he caught his mother watching him with one of her I-know-best-dear looks. She had sent Beth to dance with him. It didn't take a genius to figure out that troublemaker's ulterior motives, and they had nothing to do with saving him from that maid of honor.

Aidan sat down at an empty table where he could see Beth and Roan speaking with other people. Roan's hand was no longer on her waist. And the more Aidan considered it, he hadn't seen them have any sort of intimate moment. Like she'd said: she was only here because she owed him a favor.

But he wasn't ready. As much as he hated to admit it, Fran's leaving still hurt. He didn't miss her but he remembered what that felt like to have the one you love betray you. But trying to not think about Bethany Spinner was like pushing water uphill.

He looked around at the couples. Some dancing, some drinking, others flirting. There was one particular couple, friends of the family Connor and Darcie O'Brian, who always looked like they were having a secret conversation that nobody else could hear. Beth was speaking to them now, smiling and nodding. Darcie was an American so Beth was probably pleased to not have to try so hard to understand them.

Maybe he wasn't ready.

But there was no reason he couldn't show a friend around Ireland.

Aidan pulled a pen and a small pad of paper from his breast pocket. Normally, he would use this paper for notes or ideas about a book, today he was writing a very different note. On it he scribbled his phone number along with a message comprising one simple word: Stay.

Aidan made his way to the table where her purse hung off the back of a chair and dropped the note inside.

He was a glutton. A demented glutton for punishment.

Farewell Ernie.

CHAPTER
Twenty~Five

THE DRIVE HOME was quiet except Roan thought he heard a sniffle. From the corner of his eye, he saw Beth's tears glisten in the moonlight flooding through the window. Not wanting to make a scene she casually wiped them away as she watched the moonlit green lands pass by.

When they reached her house, he parked the car then walked around to open her door. She accepted his hand after she emptied her balled up fist of tissues into her purse.

Roan helped her stand but didn't release her hand. "Bethany, what's made you cry? Won't you tell me?"

"Why didn't I just fly away to some sunny island where I could flop onto the beach in nothing but a sarong, and drink until I can't feel my face while a cabana boy rubs sunscreen on my skin? That would have made more sense than this! I hate it here and Ireland hates me back! I nearly killed you, I drive on the wrong side of the road, I'm always getting rained on." She could go on but didn't.

"Bethany love, listen. Do you know how many people talk

about doing something like this but never do because they're too afraid?"

She shook her head and tears flung from her cheeks. "You're very brave to come here on your own. I'm sorry it hasn't worked out the way you had hoped but there's time to change that. You like this cottage, don't you?"

She nodded her head.

"And you met some of your neighbors tonight, did you like them? I know they liked you."

"They did?"

"Yes. In fact, I know the widower three doors down—"

"Mr. Byrne."

"That's right. He has plans to ask you to dinner."

"What? Be serious. He's old enough to be my father."

Grandfather more like. "Maybe so but he told me you were the sweetest woman he'd met since his wife died and he was going to ask you on a date."

Her tears stopped to make way for the baffled blinking.

"And Connor and Darcie O'Brian told me they planned on inviting you over."

"They said that? But they have twins at home. They haven't got time for silly me."

"Darcie was once in your shoes. I bet she sees some of herself in you and wants to help you feel more comfortable."

"She told me she came here alone and was scared too but that now she couldn't imagine being anywhere else. Darcie was really nice—and so pretty. Those green eyes of hers! She said this was their first night out since she gave birth to their twins." Beth smiled as she pictured the way Darcie and Connor looked at each other. "They really looked in love, didn't they?"

Roan agreed. "I don't know if I've ever seen another couple

look at each other the way they do." He gazed longingly into Beth's eyes. She smiled and glanced away.

She didn't know why she was even considering staying. Why should she? Because his eyes pleaded. She nodded her head. "You win. I'll give Ireland another shot. I hear it's beautiful here."

Roan chuckled which made her giggle. She was so beautiful when she smiled. Roan couldn't stand it, the rush of affection was too strong. He moved fast cupping her face in his hands and planted his mouth to her soft lips.

"I'm sorry." He backed off but she looked so beautiful in the moonlight. "You know what? I'm not sorry."

He stepped to her again and took her in his arms kissing her good and long. He kissed her the way she deserved to be kissed. At first her shoulders tensed, her eyebrows shot upward. But as his kiss deepened she opened to him, her shoulders relaxed, her eyes drifted closed, and her arms went limp at her sides.

Only after a slightly inappropriate amount of time had passed did he step back, wishing her goodnight and returning to his car.

Beth stood, holding her keys while watching him walk away into the misty night then turned and unlocked the door but before she could step inside she heard the meow of a cat. She turned around and there was a cat regal with his long snow-white fur, pink nose, and pair of small crystal blue eyes looking up at her.

"I know who you are. People have been looking for you, Mr. Jameson." She pushed the door open and the cat dashed inside.

"Were you spying on me and Roan outside? I guess you don't like him since he said he couldn't find you. Why don't you like him? He's a good kisser, and handsome, and gentle, and kind." She started brushing her hair, then realized she was talking to a cat.

Mr. Jameson paraded through the house like he owned the place. Which he did, of course. Then he raced to the kitchen doing a slide and stop on his backside to where his food dish would normally be, sat and waited. Good thing there was still some cat food in the pantry. Beth opened a can and placed some on a saucer. He ate that then wanted more, and more, until he'd devoured the entire can of food. Then, he took a drink from the bowl of water she placed down for him, rubbed against her leg in thanks then made his way to her bed, where he parked his royal rear end in the center of the pillows.

"Seriously? The middle? Where am supposed to sleep?"

The cat can't hear her but he opens one eye and she knows that he knows. Maybe he reads lips?

"Poor little guy. You probably ran away because you were scared and sad that your mommy died. Where have you been sleeping? And eating? You're no outside cat. You're a spoiled house cat." He opened both eyes. Yeah, he knows all right. Beth let her hair down and undressed, talking to her new roommate all the while. "I'm kind of like you. My grandma died and I ran away scared and sad. I'm still scared and sad. I'm sleeping in a place that isn't my home—it might as well be a big dark dangerous forest like you've probably been in. Super. I'm kindred spirits with a cat. A cat that is deaf but I'm talking to anyway like he can read lips." She looked at his handsome face with blue eyes. Even the Irish cats had those sparkling blue eyes.

"Listen I'll take care of you, if you share the bed with me." She patted her hand on the other side of bed. Mr. Jameson yawned, went to her hand, and curled up, purring as she stroked his head.

After changing into her pajamas, she called Lauren.

"Hey, Klutzy! How was the wedding?" In other words, Lauren wanted to know how the wedding went being stuck between two men that clearly had a thing going for Beth. Lauren did a little excited dance while sitting on the sofa.

"It was good. It was beautiful too. You should have seen that hotel! You can't understand a thing anyone says there but it was so pretty, who cares? And the food was so delicious, and the—"

"I want to hear about Aidan and Roan!"

Beth knew that. She just felt like teasing her. "Roan is a gentleman, not a poor dancer, and a really nice kisser."

Lauren squealed. "He kissed you? When?"

"Just now, on the doorstep."

"Did you swoon? That sounds swoon-worthy."

"I think I might have done a little swooning but it sort of felt like a pity kiss. Maybe not, I don't know. I was upset. There's more."

"More? What more?"

"Roan asked me to stay here in Ireland a while."

"He did? Lauren restrained herself from screeching. "Are you going to?"

"Wait, there's more. Aidan asked me to stay too."

Now Lauren sat up straight. "He did? What did you say?"

"I didn't say anything …"

"Did you spend more time with Aidan at the wedding?"

"We danced, I met his sister, who at first was a real …"

Lauren filled in the word for her. "Bitch?"

"Yeah. But turns out she's pretty nice, I met his parents, nice people. His mom asked me to dance with Aidan so he wouldn't have to dance with the maid of honor who was pretty handsy."

"So do you think he's interested in you?" Lauren thought Aidan was interested. Very interested. Purring came through the line. "Beth, what's that sound?"

"That is Mr. Jameson, the cat that ran away. He was there on the doorstep when I got home tonight."

"The cat that's been missing for weeks that Roan's been looking for just came up to you?"

"Yeah, isn't that funny? You should see him. He's so handsome with his blue eyes and so affectionate."

"Are we still talking about the cat?" Beth was getting more action in Ireland than she'd seen in a year at home. And she had described some of the country she'd seen on the drive and couldn't stop saying how beautiful it was. That was a far cry from the miserable, lonely, and depressed Beth she had spoken with a few days ago. Lauren whipped out her deck of tarot cards and shuffled then pulled the first card then the second, she didn't bother flipping the other. Biting her lip, she thought for a moment. She had probably meddled enough. "You sound tired. You don't have to decide tonight if you want to cancel your flight. Sleep on it."

"You think I should stay, don't you?"

"Yeah, I do. But not just because of the guys."

"There are no guys. Just Roan. I didn't even realize he thought of me like that until tonight."

Sigh … Klutzy, Klutzy, Klutzy … They could address her inability to read men later. "You said yourself the weather has changed. You could stay another few days and get out there and maybe enjoy yourself. You flew all the way out there, and you may never go again. Do you really want to come home after a couple of lousy weeks when you had the opportunity," not to mention the invitations, "to maybe experience something great?" Lauren paused before bringing out the big guns. Sure, Lauren could lie about Beth's flight being cancelled, but that would only keep her there for another day or two before she caught on. No, she had interfered enough. But there was more than one way to crack an egg. Gram could make Beth stay there and give her trip another chance. "Besides, Gram wanted this for you. Don't you think you owe it to yourself to give it one more shot?"

Mr. Jameson rubbed his soft, fuzzy cheek to Beth's, purring loud as a large diesel truck while she stared at the TV screen where a rerun of *Murder, She Wrote* played. Angela Lansbury was sitting at her typewriter in her reading glasses writing her latest novel.

That really was a good show. Beth had forgotten how much she liked it.

What could a few more days hurt? Two days ago, she would have said that crucifixion would be less painful than staying another day in Ireland. But the countryside she'd seen today was beautiful.

Beth would never admit, not out loud anyway, that Aidan's note surprised her. Nearly everything about him that day had surprised her. There was even a moment when she had thought he might be flirting with her. But, looking back on it now, he was likely only being nice.

And Roan's invitation to stay had been so generous. And that kiss …

If the weather turned soggy again, at the very worst she would stay in a cozy, warm cottage, cuddling with a cat and watching TV. There were worse ways to spend your vacation.

That's what Roan would call couch-melting relaxation.

"Would you cancel my flight?"

Did Lauren know or did Lauren know? High five! She smiled and lied through her teeth, "Of course I can!" She clicked her mouse a few times and punched on a few keys just for effect. "Done!"

CHAPTER
Twenty-Six

THE FOLLOWING day Beth woke up to Mr. Jameson laying on her chest, pushing her eyelids open. The sun was up, he was up, she should be up. Beth blinked a few times. As the white fluffy face came into focus she scratched his cheeks and throat as he purred and purred. If she was going to stay a while longer they would need to figure out another method of getting her up in the morning. After a morning snuggle, she threw over the covers and got out of bed with Mr. Jameson leading the way.

Beth yawned and stretched like the cat at her feet then looked at the clock on the wall. Mr. Jameson stretched from his front toes to the tip of his tail.

She reached the bathroom then turned on the shower and smiled when the steam rose.

Mr. Jameson followed her and sat on the edge of the sink, then as Beth stepped under the spray he howled. And cried. And howled.

Apparently, Mr. Jameson didn't like her being under that shower spray. Or he was hungry.

Either way His Royal Highness would have to wait.

Once in the kitchen, the regal Mr. Jameson situated himself in front of the cat-themed placemat on the floor and waited while Beth prepared a saucer and cat food. Having smelled his food Mr. Jameson grew impatient and meowed loudly, and with many octaves, as he stood on his two back feet, begging. Before she placed the plate onto the floor, he had his face in it.

Beth snickered. He wasn't so dignified now, was he?

"I need to go to the store and get you more food." She had found two cans of his food, his empty litter box and a bag of cat litter but those wouldn't last. She opened the refrigerator and brought out the last two eggs from Roan. "I need eggs, and juice and—I'm talking to a cat." Mr. Jameson didn't seem to mind. Then again, he was deaf. Beth shrugged her shoulders and continued telling him her grocery list while she scrambled her eggs and was so relaxed, she didn't notice that the thought of going out into the big bad world didn't seem so scary today. What a difference a day makes.

———

With her shopping list in hand, Beth passed through the doors of the grocery store, pulled a cart out of the line and headed for the refrigerated section. After walking up and down the aisle she was ready to throw her hands up. How hard could it be to find eggs? Not seeing them anywhere she gave up and moved on to the pet section. She rounded a corner, avoiding a tall display of canned tomatoes and yelped when she crashed her cart into another.

"Spinner! I should have known," Aidan teased, shaking his head.

"Are you following me? I've been to this grocery store twice and both times here you are."

"I'm working here doing research for a book. It's about a couple that fall in love after she crushes him under an avalanche of canned tomatoes."

"The lost cat of Roan's grandmother that you asked about? He came back last night!"

"Figures it would come to you. So, you've started your crazy cat lady collection?

"I'll wait till I get back to Minnesota to start that. He's very friendly only he was sleeping on top of my head and I startled him."

"Did you get home okay?"

"Of course, I did. Roan is a nice guy," she said indignantly. What exactly was he trying to say? He'd better not be implying she was loose again.

"I didn't mean to imply that he wasn't." Sure, he did. Hey, Roan was a friend but they weren't close. All's fair in love and war. "I was only asking after your welfare." Like hell he was. "Did he enjoy the wedding?"

"I think so, yes. I don't know how thrilled he was that I caught the bouquet. His eyes went a little too round, you know?"

"Maybe he's allergic to flowers or he's just not ready to get married. You can't fault the guy for that. So, you're buying groceries ..." He examined the items already in her cart, most of it was cat food.

"Do you know where the eggs are? I can't find them." There were two hundred kinds of yogurt but no eggs.

"That's because you're thinking like an American. Here, eggs are fresh and kept on the shelf." He led her to the eggs and as promised, they were on a shelf. "Did you enjoy the wedding? You know, aside from my sister being my sister?"

"Yes, I did."

"Did you find my note?"

"Yes, I did." She tried so hard to stay cool but her phony, uninterested face cracked into a smile.

"Does this mean you're staying?"

"Yes, I am."

Aidan grinned a little and nodded.

"I had Lauren cancel my flight. I figured I would give my trip another shot. Like you said, why come all the way here only to give up?"

You're up Turner, you got her to stay. Now what? "In that case, how would you like to see the places from the book? I would take you myself."

Her excitement couldn't be contained. "Really? You would do that?" Maybe this is why he wanted her to stay. Her heart sunk a little but she reminded herself that he hadn't actually showed genuine interest in her. They were friends, and that was enough.

"Sure, I would. We're friends, aren't we? How is tomorrow morning? We'd be gone all day."

Was he kidding? All day getting a personal tour of the places from her most favorite book ever? She replied with as much self-control as a chocoholic in a candy shop. "Tomorrow is good. Do I need to bring anything?"

"Just yourself, but wear comfortable shoes." He looked down at her feet and saw her toes wiggling like crazy inside her sneakers. "Now, I owe my mom dinner so I have to get going." He took a step then turned to her with a smile. This time, he wasn't running off. "See you in the morning, Spinner."

Yowza was that man hot when he smiled a big toothy grin. Earth to Bethany! He's not for you. Blink! Focus!

Aidan cooked? Beth looked at the contents of Aidan's cart. Among other things, he had fresh herbs, two varieties of Italian cheese, several cans of tomatoes, three kinds of meat … For the first time in her life, she wished she wasn't allergic to tomatoes.

With a smile that met her eyes, she continued down the aisle in the opposite direction as Aidan. Yes, this trip was definitely turning around.

She then realized she'd forgotten her eggs and nearly turned back to fetch some when she spotted a dozen resting in her cart beside a loaf of bread. Beth smiled to herself, Aidan must have placed them there. She opened up the lid to inspect them. They were brown, just the right size, and none were broken.

CHAPTER
Twenty-Seven

BACK AT THE blue cottage with the bright yellow door, Beth stepped inside with two bags of groceries in tow and was greeted by a hungry Mr. Jameson.

"Were you a good boy while I was gone?"

The regal, white, long-haired Prince told her all about how good he was, and more, while she put away the groceries. Being deaf, his voice was louder than most cats and had quite the range but since he purred all throughout his commentary, she figured that whatever he was telling her was nothing but good things.

She opened a can of cat food and served it to him in a saucer on his mat then stood, looking out to the garden through the glass door. What a pretty day it was.

Beth stepped out into the sunlight and turned when a knock sounded at her front door.

"I'm back here!" she called out. She opened the gate as Roan rounded the corner. "I thought it would be you," she said with a bright smile.

From behind his back, he pulled a fresh bouquet of wild flowers. "I thought I should check on you. After last night and all."

Beth held the flowers to her nose, taking in the scent. Roan was very thoughtful. "I'm better now and you'll be happy to hear that I decided to stay a little longer."

She led him into the kitchen so she could put the flowers in one of the many colorful vases around the kitchen.

Roan had hoped she would stay. "In that case, would you like to have dinner with me tomorrow?"

"I would but I can't. Aidan is taking me on a drive."

Aidan had wasted no time. Roan's suspicions of Beth and Aidan were heightened. "Is it a date?"

"No, it's nothing like that. Aidan's just showing me the places from his book."

There was no question to how much she was looking forward to the tour, and he believed her when she said it wasn't a date—but that inkling he'd had at the wedding, when he didn't know if they hated each other or were madly in love—moved forward in his mind. If that inkling was true, then he had competition.

Being an easygoing guy, Roan decided to take it day by day. After all, she may be gone in a week.

But there was no reason not to make the most of that time.

He stared at Beth as he placed his elbows on the countertop. She didn't seem like the lying type. If she said there was nothing between Aidan and her he could believe her. But he still couldn't shake the feeling that something more was going on between them. He'd noticed how she looked at Aidan. Moreover, he'd noticed how Aidan looked at her.

It was now Roan decided there was only one way to find out: date Bethany Spinner.

Oh, dear, what a shame. It would be a sacrifice, of course, but a sacrifice he was willing to make.

"I have good news."

"Tell me."

"Your grandmother's cat is here."

"Mr. Jameson? How did you catch him?"

"I didn't catch him. He came to me, trotted inside, and has been living the life of Riley ever since."

Roan chuckled. It figured that cat would simply waltz up to Beth when it avoided everyone else.

"Roan, would you mind if I used some of your grandmother's painting supplies?"

"You paint?"

"No, I thought I might try."

"I'll say yes on one condition." Arms crossed, he eased close, placing his shoulder beside hers. "Let me see what you paint no matter what you think of it."

"Deal."

"And, have dinner with me Wednesday night?"

Beth's pulse jumped and she turned her face to his, his warm breath whispered by her mouth. "Okay."

They remained still, just breathing. Watching, waiting. Her pulse quickened and her lip quivered. Why wasn't he kissing her? Was he waiting for her to move in? Because—

His phone rang from inside his pocket. By the tone he knew it was his sister.

Beth blinked. "Aren't you going to answer that?"

"It can wait." He looked over face. Her cheeks rosy, her lips waiting. He remembered the taste of those lips ...

He leaned in, could already feel that first spark of skin on skin, then ... felt the cashmere softness that was unmistakably Mr. Jameson.

Mr. Jameson had decided Roan had seen quite enough of his new mistress so he did what any loyal cat would do: he tickled his fluffy tail between their faces.

Roan and Beth split apart, pulling fur off their mouths and blowing the white fuzz away.

"I told you he doesn't like me. I don't know why."

Attempting to muzzle herself, Beth covered her mouth. But Mr. Jameson now addressed Roan, yelling at the top of his lungs.

"I have my own cat at home and she loves me! But not His Majesty here!"

His Majesty turned around and farted, then all but pointed his tail at the door, ordering Roan to leave. Beth had never seen a more animated cat and exploded into laughter.

Roan didn't think laughter like that could come from morose Beth but it was music to his ears. "I'll be off now then, love. Have fun painting and I'll see you Wednesday." He opened the glass door and stepped outside, then looked back over his shoulder. "And enjoy your tour tomorrow."

Beth was laughing so hard she couldn't speak, so she waved goodbye.

Mr. Jameson fell mute the moment the door clicked into place. Which, if it were possible, made Beth laugh even harder.

She had a chaperone!

Once she composed herself, which (gracious me) took a few good minutes, she scooped Mr. Jameson into her arms and snuggled him. "Does this make you my knight on a white horse?" Goodness, she hoped not.

She wasn't ready for the Crazy-Cat-Lady-party-of-two phase.

She placed Mr. Jameson down then made her way to the art

studio with him trotting along beside her. No princess should be without her gallant knight.

When she opened the door sunlight flooded in and she had a view of the garden wrapping around the house. She could see why Grannie had made this her art studio. To the right was her easel, resting beside an empty stool. Behind it were blank canvasses of various sizes and shapes. Beth selected the smallest canvas there was, which was still 24x24 inches. Hey, she wanted to try painting so, like Gram would have said, "Go big or stop wasting my time!"

Beth placed it on the easel then, after putting on Grannie's well used smock and selecting a palette of paints, sat on the stool.

CHAPTER
Twenty-Eight

AIDAN ARRIVED at Beth's house eager to get a start to their drive. It had rained overnight, but it was a now bright day. However, rain was returning and might even cut their tour short so he wanted to get going as quickly as possible. Hopefully she was ready to go. It would be a shame if their day was cut short.

He knocked on Beth's front door as it flew open. There was Beth all dressed and ready to go, holding her purse in one hand and a rain jacket in the other. She would not get caught in the rain on the day of her personal tour.

"Good morning, Cupcake!"

"Good morning, Sweetums!"

"I'm excited!" she said as racing to his car, she nearly knocked him down.

"As excited as a dog with two tails?"

"Maybe." Definitely! Aidan rushed to open her car door before she did so herself. It had been a long time since she had been shown real courtesy by a man, and now she had two courteous gents.

Figures. When it rains it pours.

She buckled her seatbelt and politely placed her hands in her lap. If she didn't she was liable to wave them in the air.

Aidan slid into the driver's seat and started the engine. "All set?"

She nodded.

"Now, would you like to know where we're going first or do you want to be surprised?"

"Surprised."

———

Beth stood beside Aidan, shoulder to shoulder, on the side of Geokaun Mountain overlooking the jagged coastline below. She could see across Dingle Bay, where she had an unparalleled view of the majestic Kerry Mountains and the wild blue ocean that stretched to the horizon.

This was magnificent.

Beth spoke in a reverent tone. "Aidan, I would say there are no words but you found the words." She recited the words from his book. "Untamed, treacherous, unforgiving, achingly beautiful."

"Well remembered. I bet you know my book better than I do."

"This place, it's old. It feels like it knows."

"Knows what?"

"Everything. Everyone. Can we stay here awhile?"

"We can stay here for as long as you like." He wanted to tuck her curls behind her ear so he could see her eyes more clearly. Then she turned her head toward him, smiled and blinked back tears of pure joy.

Aidan had forgotten what it was to appreciate beauty until now.

They had been to a beach where she found sea glass among the boulder-sized rocks on the shore, and seen dinosaur footprints forever preserved in stone. And stretched before her was a shade of blue only seen in dreams. She took picture after picture, knowing that none would compare with the real thing, decided this was the view one had to feel deep down in their soul to remember.

———

Just as Aidan had feared, the rain came and he was forced to cut their day together short and take Beth home. He would have offered to make her dinner or take her out but during the ride, she had mentioned wanting to paint. She said their trip had inspired her. Although part of him wanted to spend more time together, and he thought he deserved a pat on the back for admitting it, he too had been inspired and was eager to drop her off.

But not so eager that he wouldn't at the very least walk her to her door. What sort of gentleman would he be if he didn't?

Aidan pulled his umbrella from the backseat and met Beth at her car door, then walked her to the bright yellow door. Once they were under the cover of the overhanging roof he lowered his umbrella and waited for her to unlock the door.

Once it was unlocked, she clumsily turned into him. Being much too childish to simply come out and admit his feelings, Aidan possibly—maybe, perhaps, there's no proof of it, but—he might have deliberately stepped into her way.

He didn't care how juvenile that was. It got him a few moments of holding her in his arms.

"Sorry about that."

"This is what we do, isn't it? Fall into each other's way?"

He'd said it with gentle amusement, not irritation. "Yes, I guess we do. Want to come inside?" she asked.

"Sure." Aidan passed through the door, into the familiar living room. "It's exactly how I remember it." He spotted the white cat curled up in the middle of the sofa. "Here's the orphan Prince." He stroked Mr. Jameson on the head. The cat opened one eye as a warning: Aidan had precisely two seconds to get his filthy hands off of him. How dare he wake him up? You don't just go around waking up sleeping cats! Eejit.

Aidan took the hint and kept moving and followed Beth into the kitchen where she poured them each a glass of iced tea.

"You know, you could be hanged for this here," Aidan said as he sipped the forbidden cold tea.

Beth giggled. "Why don't they ice their drinks here?"

"It doesn't really get hot enough to need a cold drink here. At least, not like back home."

Beth cocked her head. Made sense.

"I'm sorry I wasn't able to take you everywhere today." He was as sorry about that as he would be winning the lottery. This gave him a more than perfect reason to spend more time with her. "I could take you out tomorrow, if you're free?"

The everyday, considerate, unselfish Bethany Spinner would have said something like "No, I couldn't possibly impose again. This has been really nice, thanks." But, this was Ireland Beth and she had just had one of the best days of her life and darnit if she didn't want more! "Really? Okay! Same time?" That didn't sound too eager, right?

Aidan nodded. "Same time tomorrow." He finished his iced tea, thanked her, then ducked out the back door.

A now giddy Beth was bouncing up and down in the

kitchen. Everything Aidan showed her that day was amazing! So amazing that it made up for every miserable day she'd had there in Ireland. Lauren was right. Beth needed to stay a little longer. And speaking of Lauren, Beth needed to call her and tell her about her day!

Beth got her phone from her purse and dialed Lauren and was shocked when the call went directly to her voicemail. That wasn't like Lauren to turn her phone off but there were a hundred reasons the call went to voicemail. Beth would simply call again later. In the meantime, she would try her hand at painting again.

As she picked up her paintbrush, Beth pontificated aloud to Mr. Jameson.

"I don't know about this friendship thing with Aidan," she spouted at Mr. Jameson who sat on the window sill with his fluffy tail swaying back and forth. "I've never really been friends with a man before but I really like him. He's nice and funny and attentive." The cat looked at her and cocked one ear. "Yes, I know, I feel a but coming too, Mr. Jameson." Beth sighed and swiped some blue onto the canvas. "What about Roan, you ask? He's nice, and so generous, and handsome too. There isn't anything bad I can say about Roan. But he feels more like a friend than a boyfriend." The cat sat up to yell at a bird outside. "I know, I said he was a good kisser and he is, but there weren't any fireworks, you know? Then again, love isn't necessarily about fireworks." Beth dabbed some white paint here and some green there and continued her one-sided conversation.

"When I was ten years old, just before my parents died, I remember getting up at night for a drink and I saw them curled up on the sofa. Mom was laid out stretching her back saying how tired she was. Dad handed her a glass of wine and sat at the foot of the sofa and then he slipped her socks off and rubbed her feet. Then he asked her about her day. It wasn't long before he had her forgetting all her troubles. They looked so comfortable together … It's funny, the things you remember."

CHAPTER
Twenty-Nine

BETH SAT BACK on the stool in front of her painting. A smudge of blue paint across her cheek, a smudge of green down her nose, a swipe of brown here, another of yellow there. A paint brush dangling from her hair. The picture was hideous. She had seen horror films with more attractive scenery. She had tried to paint the view of the sparkling sea from the cliffs. What she actually did was paint something that looked more like Dante's seventh circle of Hell.

It wasn't pretty.

She was absolutely horrible at painting!

But man, was it fun!

As she shook her head laughing a knock sounded at the front door. She was in no condition to see anyone. What would they think? Meh, who cares! Beth opened the door and smiled. "Hi Roan. Come on in. I see it stopped raining."

Roan shoved his hands in his pockets and nodded, trying desperately not to laugh. "Yeah, it quit about an hour ago." He couldn't look at her. It was too funny. How did she manage to get a paintbrush stuck in her hair? Was there any paint on the canvas or did she roll in it herself?

It was more than obvious that Roan was about ready to bust a gut so Beth put him out of his misery. "Aren't you going to ask what I've been doing?"

That did it. Roan barked with laughter and was quickly joined in by Beth.

"All right, I believe a promise is a promise? Let's see what you did."

She turned on her heel and led him to the art room, where she made him close his eyes and let her lead him into position.

"Okay, open your eyes! Ta-da!"

Roan hid his smirk under his fist. It was … well … you know it kind of reminded him of … it was hideous.

Beth breathed an exaggerated sigh. "You know, I always wanted to paint," she said as she stepped back to examine her, ah-hem, masterpiece.

Choking on his own laughter, Roan asked, "Why didn't you?"

"I don't know. Just busy, I suppose." Beth threw her hands up then turned to Roan. "I always thought it would make me feel like I was in a Jane Austen novel."

"And do you?"

She frowned. "No." Then she smiled wide, laughing. "It's so much better than that!"

"Are you going to keep painting, you think?"

"No. I think this might just be a something silly I did while on vacation thing."

"And they say God isn't real! I tell you."

Beth sputtered with laughter as she followed him to the kitchen. "Did you stop by just so you could laugh at me?"

"No, I was out for a walk and saw your light on so I thought I'd stop by. How was your drive today?"

"It was so amazing! We went to Valentia Island."

"That's a beautiful spot."

"It started raining though so we had to cut the day short. He's taking me out again tomorrow."

"That's nice." He wasn't sure if that was sarcastic or not but the ring was unmistakable. "Would you like some help getting that paintbrush out of your hair?"

"Yes, please."

Roan guided her over the kitchen sink where she flipped her hair under the faucet. As he washed, ran soap and water over the handful of hair stuck around the brush he said, "Listen, about dinner on Wednesday. Some neighbors were talking about having a poker night. I thought you might enjoy that. We could go if you like? Then have dinner together Friday?"

From underneath her red mane she called back to him. "I would but I'm not a very good card player."

"That's flying low and spreading it wide Bethany Anne! Don't be fooled by her innocent face. She's the most competitive person I know!"

Beth hit her head against Roan's soapy hand as she stood and turned with a gasp. "Lauren? Lauren! You're here!"

Roan covered his ears to muffle the squealing friends. There was no sense in trying to get the paintbrush out now. Those two were going to be hugging and crying for a while yet.

"Why didn't you tell me you were coming?" Beth stood back but held on to Lauren's shoulders.

"Why, so you could pick me up at the airport? I'd like to actually see Ireland before I take my life in my hands."

Roan laughed in his throat. Yes, this was definitely the terrifying Lauren he'd met on the phone.

Lauren looked over Beth's shoulder at the handsome man with a killer smile who was drying his hands, and practically shoved Beth away. "You must be Aidan! It's nice to meet you! My bestie didn't do you justice."

Roan pursed his lips and placed the kitchen towel beside the sink. No, this wasn't awkward at all! "Ah, no. I'm Roan." He held out his hand in hello.

Beth gulped. Cripes! "Lauren, you got the name mixed up."

"Ope, I did? I'm sorry!" Lauren shook hands with Roan and sized him up. So far, so good. "I would forget my own name if it wasn't on my driver's license. Ask my kids! They pretty much answer to 'hey kid.'" Before her tongue slipped down her throat any further Lauren excused herself. "Beth, I need the bathroom."

Beth pointed toward the hallway. "It's down the hall, first door on the left."

"It was nice meeting you Lauren," Roan said as she turned to leave the room.

"You too, Roan."

Being an expert navigator of awkward situations Beth kept things moving. "How about I give you a rain check on dinner?"

"I have a better idea. How about you come and bring Lauren too?"

"We'd love to!" Lauren shouted from around the corner. Like she was *actually* going to leave? As if!

Beth rolled her eyes with a huff. "We'd love to."

"Good. Right, then I'll leave you two ladies. Good night, Lauren." Roan said as he passed Lauren leaning against the wall in the living room. He turned back when he reached the door and looked at Beth. "Are you really that competitive?"

"Maybe." She said playfully.

"I look forward to seeing that." With a grin, he left, closing the door behind him and it was only a moment later the girlish screams started all over again. Roan shook his head with a chuckle and headed for home.

———

After crying, laughing, eating and then repeating it all over again, Beth and Lauren laid in bed, head to foot, with Beth on her stomach and His Royal Highness, Mr. Jameson, laying up her backside with all four legs in the air.

"He looks happy. What will you do with him when you come home?" Lauren asked, stroking the cat's belly.

"I don't know. He doesn't like Roan."

"Maybe one of the neighbors will take him?" Lauren suggested, watching the cat's paw twitch as he fell asleep.

"I hope so. I would hate to think of the little guy fending for himself." For the first time in her life, Beth knew what being alone felt like and, although she wouldn't normally say this: it sucked pickled ass. "I still can't believe you flew out here. What about the Alan and the boys?"

"Are you kidding?" Lauren looked at the clock on the wall. It was dinner time back in Minnesota. "Right now, those boys are all laying around in their underwear, eating pizza, and playing video games. They're having a great time." Lauren found some hair matted together on Mr. Jameson's belly and gently unknotted it without disturbing him. "At least the paintbrush came out without me having to cut your hair. Like that time you got maxi glue everywhere except your nail," Lauren reminisced, a hint of laughter in her voice as she patted Beth on the backside.

Beth shuddered at the memory. What a mess that was! Her fingers were stuck together, the fake nails dangled from her hair … "Those press-on nails were supposed to stay put on their own, but they never did." Beth nudged Mr. Jameson awake so she could turn over and climb under the covers. The cat barely opened his eyes when he rolled off and was asleep again the moment he landed on the soft blankets.

Lauren, struggling to keep her eyes open, yawned then reached across the bedside table and turned out the lamp. "Remember when we were young and partied like brain-dead test monkeys?"

"Yeah, and paid for it with something that gave a new meaning to hangovers." Beth snuggled into the sheets. "Besides, that was usually you, not me."

"True. You got me home safe and sound many times."

"One of us had to be the responsible one once in a while."

As the conversation drifted, Beth shared details about her drive with Aidan. The more Beth spoke, the more certain Lauren became there was something more between them than just two people who became friends on a plane. After all, Lauren had taken the same flight they had, she even flew first class, but all she got out of it was free booze, a comfortable seat, and a neighbor with a sinus infection.

"Are you sure there's nothing between you two?"

Although it was dark Beth turned her face away from Lauren. "Aidan isn't interested in me. He's just being nice. Probably looking for fodder for his next book." If Beth were truly honest, she would admit that it irked her. But she wasn't there yet. "It's fine."

It was anything but fine. Lauren pulled the covers up a little higher, tucking them underneath her arms. Beth insisted Aidan wasn't interested in anything but friendship. Maybe that was true, maybe it wasn't.

One thing Lauren was absolutely certain of: whether she wanted to admit it or not Beth had it bad for Aidan.

Lauren flew all the way to Ireland to meet Roan and Aidan for herself, ensuring she hadn't unintentionally ruined her best friend's life with her lies. So far, Roan seemed nice, and next, she would size up Aidan. But for now, all she wanted to size up was her pillow. Matchmaking was exhausting.

CHAPTER
Thirty

LAUREN WOKE up to the sound of birds chirping outside the window and a white tail dusting her forehead. She reached up and ran her hand down the cat's soft fur and moved his feather duster tail away from her face. Beside her, Beth's side of the bed was empty and cold and according to the clock it was nearly noon. Lauren sat up and stretched with a wide yawn. The house was quiet.

"Where did your new mommy go?" Lauren asked Mr. Jameson, whose reply was to stay put, fanning his tail. Great, now she too was talking to a cat. She pushed herself from the bed and dragged her jet-lagged hind end to the kitchen in search of coffee. Lauren was halfway down the hallway when she heard voices and smelled that spicy aroma she desired.

The closer she got to the kitchen the louder the voices became. One she recognized as Beth. Since it didn't sound like Beth was in any trouble, Lauren continued on her sluggish hunt for coffee.

When she reached the kitchen she could see Beth outside in

the garden talking with a man. Lauren couldn't understand anything they were saying, she couldn't even see the man's face since he had his back turned. Humph. That's okay, Lauren could be patient, especially when coffee and bagels were provided, and they were.

Lauren poured herself a cup of coffee with cream and prepared a bagel, all the while observing Beth and the mystery man. She'd given up trying to hear what they were saying when she started to eat her cinnamon raisin bagel with cream cheese. But suddenly she didn't need to strive to hear them. With their voices raised, Beth's hands flew in the air over her head. The man stepped away, then stepped back, then away and back again. Then he left, slamming the fence gate behind him and Beth stormed into the house, slamming the sliding door.

"Okay, Hoss! Wow, that was impressive! So, that was Aidan." That wasn't a question. The mystery man could only be Aidan. Lauren didn't need that coffee anymore to wake her up. This was way more exciting than caffeine.

Beth snatched a bite of Lauren's bagel and shoved it in her mouth. "How did you know that?" she asked with her mouth still full.

Under her skin Lauren was ready to blast off with excitement but you would have never known by her steady voice. She took a sip of coffee and replied, "Because you've never fought with any guy like that before. The sexual tension between you two is sizzling. Not to mention the stars in your eyes."

Beth rolled her eyes. "What? You're crazy. We're just friends."

"Your eyes were actually twinkling when you were arguing."

"They were not!"

"You think he's hot, don't you?"

"Of course not. Don't be ridiculous." *No. Maybe. Kind of. Totally!*

"Me thinks thou—"

"Me thinks you're crazy!"

Uh-huh, sure. Who was shouting right now? "Maybe, but I know what I saw. And what I saw was two people that want each other. A blind dodo could see those fireworks!" Lauren went back to eating her bagel with her elbows rested on the island, casually gazing outside. "So, what were you two fighting about anyway?"

"We weren't fighting."

"Then what were you two discussing passionately?"

Beth scrunched her nose and sneered. But when she thought about it, she couldn't remember. "I don't know. I'd left him a message saying you were here so he was inviting you out on a drive and then I don't know we were just talking regular stuff and I mentioned that Roan caught me naked in the garden and then suddenly he flipped out. It was weird."

"Weird? Is that what you're calling it?"

"Why what would you call it?"

"Jealousy."

"Be serious!"

"I am. He's jealous that Roan saw you naked and he didn't."

Beth turned and marched out of the kitchen. She didn't have time for this nonsense.

"Hey, wait! Are we still going on that drive?" Lauren hollered after her with a mouth full of bagel.

"Yes! So, get dressed!"

Lauren took the last large bite of her bagel and smiled wide as she chewed and washed her hands in the kitchen sink. She couldn't have asked for a better way to find out exactly what Aidan Turner's intentions were.

———

"Aidan what does that sign mean? The one with the jagged line on it?" Lauren asked from the back seat. The road they had been traveling had to be the narrowest, most winding, terrifying route she'd ever seen.

"I wouldn't mention those signs if I were you, Lauren. Beth here has a bad relationship with them."

Beth loathed those blue signs with the squiggly line. Her theory was that instead of it representing the Wild Atlantic Way their real purpose was showing what the roads were like. "They are markers for The Wild Atlantic Way."

"What's that?" Lauren asked.

Beth turned around in her seat. "Hell on Earth disguised as beauty."

Aidan looked at Lauren in his rearview mirror with a smirk. He had warned her not to mention those signs.

Lauren knew how to take a hint, but it was so much more fun to poke Beth on the rare occasions when she got cranky. "It's a miracle you haven't dented your car."

Beth knew when she was being goaded. "I did. On the passenger side."

Aidan chimed in. "A rock wall?"

"Small boulder."

"Yeah, there's lots of those around here." He had considered driving them through the Gap of Dunloe, but all he could picture was Beth covering her eyes in terror at the sight of the all the house-sized boulders scattered around the single most treacherous road in all of County Kerry. At least that's how Beth would see it. Especially since the river would be running fast thanks to the excessive rain of late. He had made it a point to stay away from the rivers and lakes. One look at that rushing water, no matter how picturesque, and Beth would surely fold. Since he wasn't looking to scare her into a cocoon, he had a better plan.

"Where are we going?" Lauren asked.

"Gleninchaquin Park. It isn't in the book but I think you'll like it." There was a lake that was sure to be high but it was small and the surrounding landscape was serene. He was confident it would be a winner.

He was right.

"My God! Aidan what is this place? It's …"

"Gorgeous." He said, finishing Beth's sentence.

"Yes, gorgeous."

He was looking at her, not at the mystical stone circle before them or the landscape. But she didn't notice, which was just as well, he decided. Because all he could see was her red hair blowing in the soft breeze behind her exposed face, her milky white skin, her graceful neck, which would undoubtedly lead to graceful soft shoulders. He moved his gaze back up. A smile was on Beth's lips that reached her eyes.

"This is quiet beauty." It was vast, unspoiled, and peaceful.

"Do you like it?"

"I love it. What is this called again?"

"This is the Uragh Stone Circle but what I really want you to see is behind it. Look past, see the water falling down the mountain face?"

Beth was so enamored with the wide open fields, the grazing sheep scattered everywhere and the ancient stones before them that she hadn't noticed anything else. But in the distance was a waterfall.

Lauren stayed back, taking pictures and observing. Sure, she thought the valley was beautiful but she couldn't be distracted from her mission to find out what was really between Beth and

Aidan. And don't think for one second she hadn't noticed him drooling into his socks over Beth! Lauren was so enamored watching the pair of them that she didn't notice the large pile of manure she'd plopped her foot six inches deep into until she tried to take a step, and couldn't. Gross. She never liked sheep anyway.

After Lauren got her sneaker cleaned as best as she could, they got back in the car and headed for the waterfall.

Suddenly, as if they had driven through a doorway, the land changed. They were now looking onto a lush, green meadow and graceful volcanic rock, where dozens of the cutest lambs ever seen pranced at its feet.

Beth was sure this was the Garden of Eden. "It's Paradise," she said as she looked around, and up at the waterfall.

"What?" Aidan asked.

"This place … is paradise."

Lauren, who no longer existed, quietly stepped back to let them have their moment.

Aidan's heart swelled. He'd known she would like this place but never could he have predicted she would fall in love with it as much as he had years before. This place was the inspiration for all his writing. Nowhere else had he found the serenity that enveloped him here.

But that was a long time ago and he hadn't found solace here in a long time. Not until today. He put his hands in his pockets to keep from taking Beth in his arms. "We've driven all over the ring for miles and miles and the place that you think is paradise was just down the road."

Sometimes the things we want most are closer than we think.

CHAPTER
Thirty-One

"COULD'VE HAD A V-8, ROAN," Beth said as she shuffled the deck of cards. They had been playing poker for an hour now.

Roan looked at Lauren and whispered. "What does that mean?"

"She's saying you made a stupid play."

"Bethany really is competitive! I thought you were exaggerating!" Roan's eyes were round, his face pale. Never in a million years would he have guessed that Beth had a dark side.

Lauren shook her head. This poor knucklehead didn't stand a chance. On the other hand, across the table Aidan was seated beside Beth and although he'd taken his share of trash talk instead of folding, he'd dealt it right back. The two other neighbors playing, whatever their names were didn't matter to Lauren, seemed fine so long as the whiskey was flowing. And it was.

"Hey! You two want to be left alone or are we going to play cards?" Beth was impatiently dealing the cards.

Aidan took away Beth's drink and downed it himself. "Hey!"

"Listen Cupcake, you don't need any more of that. I'm simply doing everyone here a favor."

Beth tried not to smile so wide as she did. She wouldn't tell Aidan of course but she liked it when he called her Cupcake. But that didn't mean she couldn't fight fire with fire. She snatched his glass of whiskey, downed it in one shot, then placed the empty glass in front of him. "You're up, Sweetums."

From across the table Roan had been observing Beth and Aidan teasing each other for the past hour. She hadn't ever teased him or looked at him with stars in her eyes. The sparks between those two were unmistakable.

Roan leaned close and whispered to Lauren, "Do you think something is going on between Bethany and Aidan?"

Lauren looked into Roan's eyes. What she saw wasn't a man who was heartbroken but one who was envious. The question was, how envious was he? "I do, yes, but Beth isn't a bone to fight over."

"I won't fight." It was his turn to play and he folded. "Not if we're right about Aidan. Not that I'd have the chance to fight for her. I like her but if she prefers him, she won't want me."

Lauren was relieved to hear it. "You're a good guy."

Roan took a drink and sighed. "That's the second time a woman's told me that today."

"Who else said it?" Lauren folded too and they dismissed themselves to the kitchen for a talk.

Roan leaned against the counter and crossed his arms. "I ran into an old girlfriend today. We really hit it off but she moved away for work before we got serious and now she's back." Roan's eyes lit up when he spoke of her. Lauren had a good feeling that Roan would not be alone for long. Which was a relief because although he wasn't the one for Beth, he was much too good to be alone. "Anyway, she invited me for dinner. Do you think Bethany would be angry if I went?"

From the kitchen doorway, Lauren looked at Beth and Aidan elbowing each other in a playful squabble. "No, Beth won't mind. That doesn't bother you?"

"I won't say I'm not disappointed."

"But you've been suspicious?"

"Yeah, since the wedding." Roan joined Lauren in the doorway spying. "Do you think they know?"

Normally Lauren wouldn't discuss her friend so candidly but she needed an ally to bring those two eggheads together before everyone grew old and died. "I think they know but need a little push and Beth won't like that. I've already pushed." Lauren looked at Roan with guilt and shame painted on her face.

"What did you do?"

"What are you two talking about?" Beth asked barging in between them. The game had ended.

"What?" Lauren asked innocently.

"I know that face."

Lauren needed an out and fast! Luckily Roan had it. "It's the face of jet lag, love. You were enjoying yourself so Lauren didn't want to say anything but she's tired. She was just asking if I would drive her back to the house so you could stay."

Beth could relate to jet lag and couldn't blame Lauren for being tired. Although she wanted to stay, her loyalty was to her friend so she offered to call it a night and return to the house with Lauren.

Lauren was quick to reply that all she really wanted was a

hot shower and a soft bed and there was no reason Beth needed to cut her evening short for that. Before Beth could make any more fuss Roan hustled Lauren out the door and into his car.

Phew! That was close!

CHAPTER
Thirty-Two

BETH AND LAUREN were in bed watching *Murder, She Wrote* when Beth's phone rang. Lauren, who was on her stomach with the cat laying up her backside with all fours in the air, looked at Beth who was so engrossed in the mystery she hadn't heard the ringing. Lauren didn't need to look to know who would be calling at this time of night.

Beth finally answered and when she heard Aidan's voice suddenly whoever the murderer was didn't matter one bit.

Lauren muted the television and waited. Beth didn't say much and the conversation was hardly a minute long before she was up and out of bed and scrambling to get dressed.

"What's going on?"

"Aidan is coming over. He says there's something we need to see."

Lauren highly doubted that he actually wanted anyone beside him but Beth so she cuddled a sleepy Mr. Jameson close and pulled up the covers. "You go. I'm too tired."

"Are you sure?"

Lauren was absolutely positively sure!

Beth was so excited that she tripped pulling up her jeans and cut her knee. That would need a minute to clean up. Oh, Klutzy …

But Beth's little accident provided just the opportunity Lauren needed to take Aidan aside and set him straight. She didn't have much time so she shoved him outside the door, closed it and spoke quickly and directly.

"What are your intentions?" Lauren demanded.

"What?" Lauren really was terrifying.

"Never mind, just listen. Beth is the kind of friend who will sew a quilt by hand for your newborn even though she stabs herself constantly and has to keep washing out the blood stains. But she sews it anyway because she knows how much you want a Winnie the Pooh-themed nursery and wants to do something extra special."

"She did that?"

"Yes. I didn't know that many bandages could fit on one hand. Bless her. My point is, Aidan, if you let her, she will pour more love on you than you probably deserve because that's Beth. She loves and forgives easily. Too easily sometimes. But she won't wait around for you. I won't let her. So, piss or get off the pot!"

Aidan stammered, and blinked, then stammered and blinked again. Just as he was about to reply, Beth opened the door. "There you are, Lauren. Are you sure you don't want to come?"

"Yes, I was just thanking Aidan for inviting me." Lauren raised her eyebrows at Aidan. "You two crazy kids have fun."

Aidan placed his hand on the small of Beth's back as she passed by and walked her to the car.

"Are you going to tell me where we're going?" Beth asked once they were in the car and on their way. Aidan had practically torn out of the driveway.

He didn't tell her where they were going. He only smiled.

Thirty minutes later he parked the car in the middle of a very dark nowhere and told her to close her eyes. He came around and guided her out of the car with his hand over her eyes. When he had her right where he wanted her, he dropped his hand to reveal the ink black sky lit with a billion bright stars.

"Aidan! I've never seen so many stars in all my life!"

"This is a dark sky reserve because there is so little artificial light. On a clear night like this, I swear you can see to infinity. It's one of my favorite places."

And he had brought her. Beth gazed as shooting stars flew across the sky, one after another. It was the most magical place she'd ever seen.

"It's so quiet. It's like I can hear the stars twinkling." She couldn't stop looking up at the vast splendor. Then again, every place Aidan had shown her was splendid. It was all like a dream. A dream she didn't ever want to forget.

A million stars reflected in her eyes as she gazed at the diamond-lit sky. Dammit if he wasn't head over heels in love with Beth. He hadn't been able to stop thinking about her. No matter how hard he'd tried she filled his brain and his heart with her delightful laugh, her kindness, the look in her eyes when she got angry. She didn't know it but it was that look that drove him wild.

Well, there were worse things. No matter what happened, he wouldn't ever forget the smile on her face right now. "You know, Beth, I, I …"

"What is it?" she asked, not taking her eyes off the sky.

"Beth, do you remember your list of regrets?"

"My what?"

"On the plane you told me the things you regret."

Beth looked at him and nodded thoughtfully.

"You've never seen the Grand Canyon. You've never had a one—"

Okay! We all know what she'd never had. "I would like to point out that I didn't think I would ever see you again and I was drunk."

"Point taken. Well, one of them was that you've never seen a meteor shower." The starlight reflected in his eyes and something changed, shifted, and grew as a meteor shot across the sky.

"Aidan, this is more than incredible. It's more than words can say. Thank you for bringing me here. There's nothing to describe this beauty."

Beth was staring at the stars, Aidan was staring at Beth. "I can think of one word."

"What's that?"

"Bethany."

That got her attention.

He reached for her, closing the distance between them.

It had taken so long to find her, he wanted to rush in, but she deserved soft, slow romance.

His fingertips feathered down her cheek and her breath caught when he cupped the back of her neck, tipping her head.

Aidan leaned in, intending to whisper sweet nothings in her ear. "Ouch" was not the word he'd intended to say but it's usually the word used when headbutted by Bethany Spinner.

A glittering meteor blazing across the sky now stole his thunder. Thanks a lot, Copernicus.

"Are you okay? I'm so sorry! Beth looked closely at his face, something was on his skin. "Aidan! Your nose is bleeding!"

Nurse Spinner quickly removed her shawl and used it to pack his nose, while she ordered him to pinch it and not tip his head back.

Yep. Romantic moment officially ruined.

Well, he had wanted to see stars.

After assessing that his nose was not broken, Beth drove them home without any trouble—except grinding the first gear. And second. And third. He was fairly certain the transmission had dropped out, and if it hadn't, if he didn't intervene it soon would.

Finally, Aidan couldn't take it anymore. His nose wasn't bleeding anymore, there was nothing holding him back. "Beth, pull over for a minute, would you?"

She pulled over and he got out of the car and walked around to her door. "What are you doing?"

"I'm flexing my male dominance by driving." In other words, he wanted to live long enough to see where this relationship would go—which wouldn't be far if they ended up at the bottom of a ravine.

Once they arrived back at her cottage, he walked her to the door. They lingered under the porch roof, gazing into each other's eyes. This had been a perfect night. Or it would have been if she hadn't given him a bloody nose. But that was a minor detail. Aidan looked at Beth with as much, if not more affection, then he had an hour before. If his face wasn't such a mess he would pick up where they had left off. But it was, so he didn't. That would be something to look forward to.

It was time to call it a night but he couldn't leave her without asking one thing burning his brain. "I have a quick question."

"What's that?"

"A meteor shower, the Grand Canyon, painting, those regrets I can understand but why do you want to ride a goat?"

She grinned and looked up and away. "Goodnight, Aidan," she said as she opened the door and stepped inside.

"Goodnight, Beth."

CHAPTER
Thirty-Three

IN THE WINDOW, Lauren observed Beth seated on the bench by the yellow door, enveloped by flowers and sunlight. Two days had passed and Aidan seemed to have vanished. Not that Beth held it against him, but Lauren sure as hell did! So what if their evening had unraveled into a complete disaster? His nose wasn't broken and Beth had driven them home safely—more or less. It wasn't Beth's fault. Accidents happen!

Yet, there Beth was, sulking and wallowing in self-pity, resembling nothing so much as a lovesick teenager. And that was Lauren's fault.

Lauren closed the curtains and turned away. This wasn't what she wanted for Beth, and Aidan obviously wasn't the man she thought he was. It was time to return to Minnesota but first, she owed her friend an apology.

She went outside and joined Beth on the bench. "Are you ready to go home?"

Beth stared at the ground and nodded.

"Me too. I'll get us on the first flight home. But, first there's something I have to tell you. It's about your flights."

"The cancelled ones?"

"That's just it." Lauren turned her head to face her friend. "I never cancelled them because I never booked them."

Beth eyes shifted from confusion, to understanding, to blazing mad. "Why would you do a thing like that?" she shouted.

"I thought you needed more time here!"

"Why? I was miserable and all I wanted was to come home!" Beth stood up and started to pace. "Oh, I get it! To see if things worked out with my hunky landlord? Jeez! You're unbelievable sometimes, you know that?" Beth swung the yellow door open and slammed it behind her.

Lauren chased after her, apologizing. "It wasn't like that! Okay, maybe it sort of was. Roan was really nice! Sue me if I wanted you to stay a couple days to see if maybe you had found someone?" Beth whirled around in a puff of steam but Lauren didn't back off. "Come on, you have to admit. You met in a storm, he generously offered you this house, he wasn't scared off by your clumsiness!"

Their fight was rudely interrupted by Aidan bursting through the front door. He'd heard their shouting from the car. "Hey, hey! Let's just get a load of mud in here so you two can really go at it! What are you two fighting about?"

Beth twirled around and focused her fury up at Aidan's eyes. One had a purple ring underneath. Beth nearly burst into tears at the sight of him but not for the reasons he wanted. She was angry and it was all his fault! She stomped across the floor intending to have it out with him once and for all but Lauren beat her to the punch.

"You've got some nerve, dickhead! Where the hell have you been?" Lauren charged him and he stepped back.

"I—"

"Well? We're waiting!"

He looked over Lauren's shoulder at Beth. "I'm sorry—"

"You're sorry? You're sorry? You're going to be!" Lauren shouted.

"Let me handle this, Lauren. Let him speak," Beth ordered. Lauren clamped her mouth shut and stepped away from Aidan. If he thought she was scary wait until he got a load of Bethany Spinner with a broken heart. Lauren turned her nose in the air and went outside.

"Beth, I'm sorry. I know I should have called. After I got home that night, I got this idea for a story and I started writing and I never stopped. It's the best I've written in a long time and I have you to thank."

In his hand was a stack of papers. Presumably the new book. And he could take that new book and his old one and shove them both right up his nose! "You've been using me? I knew it!" And just like that the light in Beth's eyes went dim.

Beth stood flexing her hand deciding what to do.

Slap him or run away?

Slap him.

She immediately made good on the thought, marched to the front door and opened it, and held her hand out, ordering him to leave.

As Aidan walked out, Lauren slipped back inside, closing the door behind her. She went toward Beth at once. "What are you doing?"

"What do you mean?"

"Go after him!"

"Why?"

"Because you're in love with him! And if you would quit stomping around like a billy goat stuck in a fence you would see that!"

"What? No!"

"Bethany Anne Spinner, you've had it bad for that man since the day you swiped him with your suitcase! Go. After. Him!"

"I can't. I'm telling you he's been using me this whole time! He told me himself."

"What did he say?"

"He said he's been writing since the other night and it's the best he's written in a long time and, well, then I yelled at him."

"Why?"

"Because he's been using me!"

"No, he has not! He said you've inspired him. What's wrong with that? A guy who had given up on everything meets you and you show him things aren't so bad." Lauren stopped shouting. "You basically gave him his life back and now he's in love with you." Lauren waited for Beth to understand and smiled as she noted Beth's dawning look of comprehension.

"I have to go after him!" She tripped over the cat but everyone was fine and she threw open the door, crashing so hard into Aidan that it knocked him down with her on top of him. Ooof.

"Hi, Cupcake!"

"Aidan! I thought you left!"

"Where would I go? I was giving Lauren five minutes to bring you around and if she didn't then I was going to wing it." Beth's hand laid on his face and he kissed the inside of her wrist that rested on his mouth. "You don't think you intimidated me so much that I would actually leave after professing my undying love for you, do you?"

"Your undying love?"

"Yes. I love you, Beth."

"You do?"

She smiled as his arms slid around her waist, up her back, and into her hair, pulling her to him.

Finally, he was going to get to kiss Beth.

Just as their lips touched Lauren stepped over their bodies. "Don't mind me. Beth, I'm leaving. I'm going to that hotel over in what's that strange sounding town?"

"Sneem!" Aidan and Beth said simultaneously.

"Yeah, that one. Sneem. And won't be back for a couple days." Wink, wink.

"Hey, Lauren, wait! Am I still a dickhead?"

She thought for a moment and smiled at the happy couple. Did Lauren know or did Lauren know! "Nah, but you're a pinhead," she said as she slid into her car.

"I can live with that."

Beth turned her face back to Aidan. "You were saying?"

"You really should have come with a warning label."

"Why? So you could avoid me?"

"No. So I could have found you sooner."

Epilogue

"I LOVE IT HERE. *It's everything you said it was in your book but …*" She looked away, knowing if she looked into his eyes, she would lose her nerve.

"But?"

"I want to go home. I'm ready to go home."

"You're leaving Ireland?"

"Yes."

He couldn't believe it. They had been so happy. "Well, I could drive you to the airport."

"No, that's okay. I'm already packed." She gestured to her car.

"You're leaving now?"

She nodded and blinked away tears.

"Are you coming back?"

"I don't think so."

"Can I call you?"

"I don't think that's a good idea."

"Why not?"

"We want different things, different lives. I happily lived my life *for someone else but now it's time I live for myself. And I know what I want."*

"But, I—"

"Please, don't say it." She raised her eyes to meet his. "I know you love me but it's not enough." She touched his cheek and he held her hand there. "Goodbye," she said in a breathless whisper.

"Aidan, this is beautiful! I laughed, I cried ..." Beth placed down the manuscript and wiped her eyes.

"Do you like it?"

"Like it? I love it! When are you sending it in?"

"I wanted you to read it first. Since you like it, I'll send it today."

"It's my new favorite book! Will you sign my copy?"

"I'll do better than that." Aidan turned to his desk where Mr. Jameson laid over top of a sheet of paper, keeping it safe and warm. So safe that he didn't want to give it up but when Aidan offered cuddles he moved. Aidan lifted the purring cat into his arms to retrieve the dedication page and presented it to Beth.

For the wonderful walking disaster that stumbled into my heart, my wife, Beth.

About the Author

Jude McLean, an American with proud Irish heritage, maintains a deep-rooted connection to the Emerald Isle, even though she can't be there as frequently as she'd like. Through her writing, she transports herself and her readers to Ireland whenever she desires, inviting them to join in the journey. When Jude isn't busy crafting captivating stories, you'll likely find her in the kitchen, concocting extravagant desserts and meals, all while joyfully serenading with a wooden spoon in hand. Known for her boisterous laughter, occasional colorful language, and an impressive ability to devour an entire cake solo, Jude assures her readers that they'll never be deprived of laughter, gasps, perhaps a tear or two, and a heartwarming smile.

Sign up for Jude's newsletter to receive insider updates, offers, and laughs.
www.judemclean.com

f facebook.com/readjudemclean
X x.com/readjudemclean
⊙ instagram.com/readjudemclean
BB bookbub.com/authors/jude-mclean

Also By Jude McLean

The O'Brians Series:

Escape, Book One

Break Free, Book Two

United, Book Three

Anne Malloy, An O'Brians Novella

An O'Brian Bride For Christmas, An O'Brians Novella

Return, Book Four Coming Soon

Surrender, Book Five Coming Soon

Other Titles:

Arse Over Irish Teacup

Made in the USA
Columbia, SC
29 June 2024

0eb0c298-622d-4d3f-86d1-eac44dfc0748R03